NAMASTE LIFE

A NOVEL

NAMASTE LIFE

Ishara Maharaj

First published by Modjaji Books 2016
PO Box 121, Rondebosch, 7701, Cape Town, South Africa

www.modjajibooks.co.za
info@modjajibooks.co.za

Editors: Fiona Snyckers and Lauren Smith
Cover artwork: Tammy Griffin
Production: Fire and Lion

ISBN (Paperback): 9781928215363
ISBN (Digital download): 9781928215370

I am not what happened to me.
I am what I choose to become.
CARL JUNG

OTHERWORLDLY DECISIONS

'What about this one, Matha?'

Lord Ganesha's elephant trunk curled and uncurled as he watched a happy family on planet Earth. Mushaka nibbled a piece of banana at his feet.

'Well ...' Mother Parvati held her golden hand over her son's shoulder. 'This home has had many happy times. They have prayed to us devotedly over the years. Very good, Putr. It appears they are the right family.'

'So dictates universal order,' Ganesha agreed. 'Many human years of good must flow into suffering before new good can follow. How else will the beings learn from past and future karma? But what about this soul we are introducing? She is on her last evolution of the human form before she can reach the supreme light. Will she have the impact that karma presents for this family? Do you think they can handle the testing? The suffering?' His trunk curled up as he entered the record in his eternal scroll of knowledge.

'They are karmasaathi. The ebb and flow of happiness is

part of their journey of human life and learning. Only earthly time will tell how this precious soul lives out the last years of her karma. But remember Putr, there are many forms of suffering on Earth – some more terrible than others – all of which are conceived and acted upon from the human mind. We cannot interfere in how their suffering comes to pass. You must let it take its course. Now, your father expects me. I will take my leave. Om Namah Shivaya.' Mother Parvati's serene face and form disappeared into her golden glow.

Her son sat still for a moment and pondered the fate of the family he had chosen. Kali Yuga was indeed a terrible time of suffering for all living beings on Earth, yet souls had to be born and reborn until they reached liberation. He hoped that the learning of the way of the universe came quickly for all of them. Having done his written work for the day, his rosy elephant trunk searched out the sweet aroma of his favourite laddoo.

OF PIGTAILS AND ROBIN HOOD

'Shirley, I'm so glad you're here! You came to visit as if you knew I needed you.'

The sun turned the satin-finished cream walls into a golden orange as it warmed Mrs Nirmala Harsingh. She was sitting in her favourite chair in her kitchen. Her childhood friend Shirley smiled at her.

'I can't believe we haven't seen each other since the girls were born, Nims. I've missed Durban so much. We could feel the warm, sticky air the moment we got out that plane. Joburg is so dry, you know. But what can you do? Ramesh's work took us there and now he doesn't want to come back here.' Shirley poured her boiling masala tea into her saucer.

'Still cooling your tea in the saucer, Shirls? Some things never change. It's so good to see you. I wish you still lived here. My life is too hectic with the girls these days.' Nirmala ran her hands through her greying hair.

'But your girls are gone so big. They beautiful young ladies now. Where they going to study next year?' Shirley had envied Nirmala ever since she gave birth to twin girls. It was always a dream of hers to have many children but Mother Lakshmi did not grant her wish.

'Shirley, remember I told you when the girls were eight and they decided to dress Ma up? Surya's bubblegum got stuck in Ma's hair and eventually she had to cut most of it. Ay ay ay, I tell you, Ma was so angry with Surya.'

Shirley giggled as she remembered the story. Even Nirmala's mother had phoned her to tell her about Surya's naughtiness.

'No, but it's not funny, Shirls. You know, Surya's tricks have got her into what kind of trouble from primary to high school. It's not a laughing matter any more. I wish she could be more like Anjani. She's been such a good girl. Always so thoughtful.' Nirmala's blood pressure was steadily rising as she thought about Surya's behaviour. 'You think I'm joking. Let me tell you how bad Surya can get then you can tell me I've got nothing to worry about or not.' Nirmala put her teacup down and cleared her throat.

Always the drama queen, thought Shirley with an inward smile.

'You know Shirls, Surya was always such a naughty girl from small. We only really noticed how bad it was when she turned twelve. She started stealing things at school and giving them to the poorer kids. Playing at being that Robin Hood on TV. And she always denied it when she got caught. She even learnt how to make an innocent face.' Nirmala put on a face to imitate her child's 'innocent' expression.

Shirley pursed her lips to control the urge to giggle. Perhaps there were advantages to not having kids after all. 'Well, don't keep me in suspense. What happened to Surya? Did she get expelled?'

'Don't make me laugh. No way would her father let them do that to his precious daughter. Of course he made things right and backed up her lies. They didn't have any proof that she stole anything so they couldn't expel her.'

'Oh my, Nims. What a story. And what about Anjani? Where was she when all this was happening?'

'You should have seen how she stood by her sister. She's another one who would defend Surya to the death. You know Shirls, I still can't believe that my two daughters from the same womb can be so different.' Nirmala undid her hair and retied it into a ponytail.

'But Nims, they finished with school now. Surely Surya has outgrown that behaviour?'

'Oh Shirls, that child finds new ways to torment me every day. High school was even worse I tell you. Except for grade 11. The whole of grade eleven went so nicely. We thought maybe Surya was finally growing up a bit. And then I got a phone call from Mr Govender's office. With shame on my face, I heard how Surya was caught on the security cameras. She was with one rubbish group of boys and you know what they were doing?' Nirmala didn't wait for Shirley to respond this time. 'They were stuffing bananas in the exhausts of the teacher's cars!'

Shirley let loose. Her laughter filled the kitchen. For a moment Nirmala joined her. Then her face stiffened as she realised it was her own daughter's shameful behaviour she had described.

'Wow Nims, you really have had some drama with Surya, hey. But shame, you'll always have those memories. Having children is not easy.' Shirley poured another cup of tea. Nirmala's masala tea was exceptional.

'What memories? More like big headaches. Grade 12 was the worst and we are just recovering from the shock of the matric dance. It was Ashok who gave them a curfew – midnight and not one minute later. He even hired a private taxi to bring them back home only because Surya was arguing with him about how silly she would look if her father picked them up from the club and how she'd die from embarrassment. That night at half past ten, Anjani came home. She told us the party was a complete waste of her time. Such an intelligent girl she is, she wasn't interested in dancing and parading for the boys even though she's so beautiful.' Nirmala picked up a picture of the girls that was stuck on the fridge.

Shirley gazed at the twins. They were indeed gorgeous in their matric dance dresses.

'But what happened to Surya, dare I ask?' Shirley continued to admire the girls.

'Oh madam left her cell phone at home. On purpose she did that, I'm sure. It was half past twelve and this girl hadn't come back. We started to panic. At one o'clock in the morning, the house phone rang. It was the police station. I thought, now what happened to my child, I was so scared. But it was nothing like that. She got caught with some university boys smoking dagga at the back of the club. Smoking! Can you believe it? This child of mine was hardly eighteen and she was smoking. She was lucky they let her off with a warning after Ashok spoke to them.'

As the afternoon sun's rays poured into the kitchen, Nirmala sighed again. She got up to clear the table.

'And now the girls are going away to study. Ashok is not gonna be there to bail Surya out of trouble. I don't think it's a good idea to send them so far away even if they are together. What would you do, Shirls?'

'Nims my dear, the girls will be fine. How will they grow

up if you don't teach them to look after themselves? Leaving the comforts of this house is the best thing for them, I think. And besides don't you want them to study further? We never got the chance to do that. They'll manage and they'll do well, Nims. They'll still have each other.'

Still, Nirmala worried about all the bad things the girls would be exposed to away from home. More rubbish boys. More dangerous drugs. More parties with rubbish boys, drugs and liquor. If Surya continued to behave the way she did, where would she land up so far away from home? Anjani was Nirmala's only comfort.

The twins were born seven minutes apart after twelve intense hours of labour. Nirmala pressed her stomach. She couldn't remember the pain any more, but she thought of her daughters as the Chinese symbol of yin and yang. They were non-identical, and it seemed that their personalities were worlds apart. Yet, despite their differences, their bond was unbreakable.

'You know you may be right, Shirls. They do have each other. I can't tell you how many times I've watched Anjani defend her naughty sister even when we all could see that Surya was guilty. If only I had a sister who loved me so fiercely.'

Shirley nodded, hoping to encourage this comforting thought. 'And you are worried, Nims? Sounds like Surya has got a guardian angel with her all the time. It's a good thing they are both going to the same university then.'

'I suppose you've got a point. If there is one thing we can count on with Surya, it's that she's never too far away from Anjani. Sometimes I wish I was also one of a pair of twins.'

KUCHLA PARTIES

'Jenny, you have so much potential, you know that?'

Surya was standing in front of Anjani's bed with her hands on her hips. She preferred to take the Indian-ness out of Anjani's name and had nicknamed her Jenny early on in their childhood. She was dressed in her favourite Guess denim skirt and dark-brown leather Nine West cowgirl boots. Under her short, cream faux-fur jacket was a slinky emerald sequined top. Her hair, like a veil of chocolate brown silk, was finished off with her natural curls at the ends. She looked like she had stepped off a New York Fashion Week runway.

'Have you ever considered modelling as a career?' Anjani said, ignoring Surya's question. She was proud and a little envious of her sister's confidence and poise.

'How about we make you over and then *you* can consider a career in modelling? I'm telling you, given my expertise in make-up and beauty and your natural good looks, you'll do much better than me in the world of fashion, Jen.' Surya flung Anjani's cupboard doors open.

'Well, it looks like we are going to have to make do with something from my wardrobe tonight. And then we need to take you shopping. Enough with the hippie stuff.' Surya held a wrap skirt from the tips of her French-manicured nails.

'Hey, that's raw silk from India. Leave it alone. And what are you talking about tonight? I'm not going anywhere. I've got research.'

Anjani closed her cupboard and put a stop to any opportunity Surya had to scrutinise her fashion choices. She didn't care much for fashion, although she loved luxurious, exotic silks and chiffons. She preferred comfort to following the latest trends.

'Research schmesearch! You're always researching. Jenny, I think there's no more research you can do. You've out-researched everything. Besides, it's school holidays. One night out won't harm your reputation as nerd of the year!' Surya was not going to back down. She led Anjani to her room.

'Why do we always have to do this? You know I hate these parties of yours. They're all pointless – everyone sitting around, trying to read each other's minds so they can suck face in a dark corner somewhere later. And then they don't even know why they did that the next morning. So pathetic.' Anjani was tired of this routine every school holiday.

'OK, I get it. You're too high and mighty to mingle with the rest of us lowlifes. But can you at least do this for me? You know Mummy and Daddy won't let me go without you being there. You're the sensible, responsible one and all that. Please, please – do it for me.' Her sister could never refuse her if she grovelled a little.

'How can you call yourself a lowlife? Hanging out with them doesn't mean you should think you're one of them!' Anjani flicked one of Surya's diamante hoop earrings.

'I'll take that as a yes, then. Thanks, sis.' Surya beamed. 'Now about your taste in fashion. What will Mrs Naidoo say if she sees you walking out the house dressed in these rags? She'll yell at you like she shouts at Sours. *Sours put your hair right! Sours put some rouge on!'*

Surya was great at impersonations. A rendition of their neighbour Mrs Naidoo's rants at her poor daughter Savathri – lovingly shortened to Sours – always cracked Anjani up.

'Uh uh uh. I will come with you as long as I get to dress myself. I don't have the legs to carry off anything in your wardrobe. But shame, poor Sours. At least Mummy doesn't do that to us.' Anjani walked back into her room. Surya followed.

'Very clever. I'll let it go tonight. But you definitely need me to take you shopping. Just let me make you over once. I promise, Jenny, you won't go back!' Surya relished the idea of making a project out of her sister's new wardrobe, mainly because it was an excuse to hit the mall.

'Makeover schmakeover. Whatever. Can I get changed now?' Anjani shoved her flamboyant sister out of her room to put on some clothes.

Ten minutes later, she stepped out in a pair of her best blue jeans and a royal purple chiffon wrap top. It was the best she could come up with for what she considered a pointless event. The only make-up she could manage was rose-tinted lip gloss and jet-black mascara and eyeliner. Surya stood in the doorway, hands back on her hips, not saying a word.

'What?' said Anjani. 'Everyone sits in the dark anyway. Why you looking at me like that?'

'Oh, my dear sister. I really must work on you. But no time now. We must get going or I'll miss out on the good stuff. And I want to chat to that new guy, Raks. He seems nice.'

Anjani rolled her eyes and followed Surya past their parents.

–

Like kuchla, the spicy mango pickle found at every Indian wedding house in Durban, these partying episodes popped up every school holiday. Surya always had the details of the best house parties and Anjani dreaded every single one of them. Not because she'd have to mingle with people that she didn't really want to, but because every event ended with Surya getting into some sort of trouble. If it wasn't a fight breaking out between two boys vying for her attention, it was some poor neighbour who'd had enough of hormonal teenagers. Anjani would have to grab her sister and plan an escape or cover-up so their parents would never hear of Surya's misadventures.

The worst episode, and Anjani's greatest cover-up to date, was when Surya disappeared from a house party in Umhlanga. Umhlanga was one of Durban's posher suburbs – the place where Indian families who made enough money to flaunt it lived. With the days of the Group Areas Act long gone, Durban North and Umhlanga Ridge – formerly 'whites only' areas – were now well populated with upper-class black and Indian families. It was also the place where far too many Durban Girls' High students aimed to find themselves one day, in a mansion overlooking the beach, with a rich doctor, engineer or accountant for a husband. Anjani felt sad and annoyed that so many talented young Indian women had no ambitions beyond marrying well. Luckily this wasn't the case for her and her sister. Both were itching to get out and explore the country, and then the world.

Posh or not, this hadn't stopped Surya from causing drama in Umhlanga when the twisted father of one of her friends hit on her at this ill-fated house party. Mr Chakkoo was instantly renamed Sleaze Bag Chakkoo. The next day, she decided to teach him a lesson in exploitation while getting something out of it for her trouble. She boldly offered to give him the night of his life if he spent the day treating her to new clothes and shoes of the designer kind. Sleaze Bag Chakkoo was eager to oblige.

Gateway Shopping Centre dominated the Ridge as the biggest mall in Durban. Lined with palm trees and water features and boasting a million shoe shops, the mall smiled on Surya that day as she collected her best friends – Louis Vuitton, Armani, Nine West and Guess. Then she tried to make off with her newfound collection by getting Sleaze Bag Chakkoo to buy her an ice-cream from the other side of the mall. The sick puppy finally caught on to her little scheme and attempted to hold her hostage. Later, an SMS from Surya begging to be rescued got Anjani and Gateway security to accost Sleaze Bag Chakkoo. Surya got away with a warning from Gateway Centre Management never to allow older men to intimidate her.

NOSY MRS NAIDOO AND HER
TRAGIC KANNA, SOURS

'Look at how they prancing up and down? Eh kanna, why you don' know where they go every weekend? You in the same class as them.'

Mrs Naidoo was talking to her daughter Savathri, better known in high school as Sours. She was leaning against the kitchen sink with the curtain pulled back just far enough so she could see what the twins were wearing. Her stomach bulged over the sink as she stuck out her generous rear. It fascinated Mrs Naidoo how Surya and Anjani's parents let them loaf every Saturday night like showgirls. But in truth , she wished for her Savathri to join them. They were beautiful and confident, and their father was proud of them. A part of her wished that Savathri hadn't inherited her lime-pickle features from Mr Naidoo's side of the family, not to mention her generous hips from Mrs Naidoo's side. It took considerable effort for Savathri to move her mouth into a smile. And her sullen mood didn't help her make friends.

'Ayo, I don' know how that mother of theirs let them go dressed like that. Look at that one's legs. And she look so big with all that make-up. Too much dark dark lipstick she got, eh. Ayo, one, one kind handbag they got also.'

Savathri peered through the window briefly. This was the highlight of her mother's weekend. But it didn't interest her. In fact, her mother's constant comparing of her to the twins was irritating. They looked gorgeous, and her mother made no effort to hide her wish that she would turn into one of them. Savathri was quite happy with her coffee-coloured skin and thick, wavy black hair. Mrs Naidoo, on the other hand, admired and envied Surya and Anjani's snowy complexions. It was always about the colour of their skin.

'Why you don't iron your hair and put on that pink outfit I bought you. I'll go outside and tell them you coming with them. At least their boy, Amos, can drop you off with them later, Sours.' Mrs Naidoo so wanted her daughter to be the talk of the neighbourhood.

'No, Ma. I can't go. I'm not invited to that party.' Savathri made to leave the kitchen before her mother could start her *when I was your age* speech. Her mother didn't understand the cliques at school. Savathri didn't belong to either of the twins' groups of friends. She was too reserved to fit in with them, and she preferred it that way. Surya was the most popular girl at school because she flashed her father's money and her good looks. Even the teachers were afraid of what came out of her mouth. Anjani was popular because of her sweet, gentle nature. She was completely different from her twin. She didn't care about money or fashion, but she was still super confident. Savathri had spoken to her once or twice. She was nice enough. But girls like the twins never hung out with ordinary people like Savathri. It was better to be a loner, she thought. If only her mother would get that.

'Tomorrow we must ask Promise where Amos took them. She always knows these things.' Mrs Naidoo's brain was scheming. 'Their mother got no shame. But she act like one high-class thing, like her shit don't stink. Hmm!'

Savathri knew how her mother detested Mrs Harsingh but wanted to be like her. She was married to one of the wealthiest men in the neighbourhood. She got to change her car every few years and their family life always seemed blissful. That was why Mrs Naidoo always poked her nose out the kitchen window, waiting for the day something would happen to change the Harsingh family's reputation. She spent hours quizzing their domestic worker, Promise, hoping some juicy titbit would have made its way through the grapevine. She was itching to find out what fancy university the twins would be sent to in the new year.

NEW BEGINNINGS BRING
MIXED EMOTIONS

The room was the first door downstairs. Anjani noticed that it was slightly bigger than all the other rooms she had walked past. As they walked in, the smell of old furniture and textbooks filled their senses. Anjani had read that, before it became a dormitory for students, this building was a prison house in the late 1800s. One thing was certain from the worn-out parquet floors and speckled plaster walls that had been painted white over and over again: this dormitory had seen many a bright-eyed female student over the years. Through the fresh coat of paint, Anjani spotted darker bits where prestik probably held up posters of whichever rock star was big that year.

Rhodes University was now the twins' home for at least the next three years. Famous for its journalism and drama departments and characterised by its historic colonial architecture, it was more beautiful than Anjani ever imagined. She'd pictured her exciting future as they drove around the campus before finding Prince Alfred House.

Nirmala was busy opening the cupboards, mumbling about giving the place a good clean before anything could be unpacked.

Anjani imagined her mother with a can of Mr Min and a yellow duster in her hands, and a lump rose in her throat as she realised that the time had come to start a new phase in her life. A phase without the constant presence of her parents. This was a mistake: leaving her family to live in a dormitory room on a campus miles away from home was wrong. But Nirmala and Ashok were standing at the door, ready to say goodbye.

'OK my sweetie. Gimme a call every week, OK?' Ashok's eyes were glassy. His fingers brushed his daughter's hair as he hugged her.

Anjani knew this goodbye was hard for him. She couldn't remember when last her father had looked at her with tears in his eyes. It must have seemed like just yesterday that she was begging him for Sugus chewy sweets and Fanta grape fizzies. She held him in silence.

'Look after yourself OK, and let me know how your sister is behaving,' her mother told her. 'You must phone me anytime, OK?' Nirmala hadn't left the building and she was already expecting the worst from Surya, who had insisted that Anjani be dropped off at her dorm room. Surya didn't want to be seen with her parents while she was scoping out male talent on campus.

Then, just like that, Anjani's parents had left her to begin her new life. She wondered why goodbyes to her mother were always focused on Surya. It was the same at every event that Surya had forced her to attend during their high-school years. Sure, her parents considered her the responsible one, but some-times she also needed to be seen as an individual with her own interests and needs. This time, her father's eyes told her that he would miss her. Their quick goodbye filled her with sadness. She grabbed a tissue from her bag and wiped her tears. The tissue smelt like home: spicy from her mother's delicious lamb curry and floral-sweet from Ma's agarbathi sticks in the prayer room. More tears ran after those thoughts.

'OK stop it now. You're here. You made the choice. Harden up!' Anjani scolded herself.

She made up her mind. It was time to step out of Surya's shadow and meet as many new people on this campus as possible. It was time to treat life as a new adventure. But first to find Gita, her best friend from high school. No adventure was complete without a trusted companion.

Anjani tidied up her eyeliner and text messaged Gita. She was the one person Anjani could turn to when she wasn't setting Surya straight. She understood Anjani and participated in her penchant for mysticism and the supernatural world. Together they had charted their times of birth in Western and Vedic astrology. They had gone for their first tarot readings together, only to find out that the gypsy was a bumbling con artist. And they stayed up late at night to summon spirits from the garden. They listened carefully when Ma spoke about her great-grandfather's spirit roaming the Main Road temple so they could pretend to be his ghost and giggle themselves off to sleep.

Deep down, Anjani believed that Gita was connected to her in a past life and so their friendship grew into an inseparable bond in this life. Much to Anjani's relief, Gita had also decided to leave home and start her young adult life in a new setting. Some of their courses would overlap this year as Gita had chosen to major in psychology.

Anjani smiled to herself as she recalled how she'd harassed the student registration department to give her more information on her courses in anthropology and geography. She wanted an early start on her assignments. Unfortunately, the staff knew nothing about the courses and she had to wait until registration week to get to her books. The first two weeks of varsity life were dedicated to orientation and adjustment. Anjani had groaned on hearing this. In her mind orientation translated into wild parties and drunken idiots.

But now she thought that maybe a change of scenery would lift her mood and allow her to meet more people. She decided to embrace the two weeks and see where the experience would take her. Her thoughts were disturbed as a scratchy voice blared over the intercom at her door – Gita.

'Anjani, where are you?'

'I'm in my room. Come down and see me! Room 15 down the stairs.' Anjani pressed the button to let Gita in and looked around to see if there was space for her best friend to sit. She wondered what Gita's room was like.

Two minutes later, Gita strolled in with two Steri Stumpies in her hand. Banana-flavoured – her favourite.

'Wow, this is a whole lot bigger than my room. But mine's newer! This furniture is ancient! How are you my friend?' Her smile lit up her entire face.

Gita Patel was a beautiful Gujerati girl – the epitome of a Bollywood beauty, fair with flawless skin, rosy cheeks, light brown eyes and pin-straight hair. She was a little shorter than the twins but had got all the attention from the Guj boys at school. Anjani admired the fact that Gita's family insisted on Gujerati school over and above normal school. Gita spoke fluent Gujerati. It helped that her whole family code-switched between English and Guj. In the Harsingh household, Bollywood's most famous couple, Abishek Bachan and Aishwarya Rai, spoke Hindi for the whole family. Bollywood movies ruled the TV screen most weekends. Ma's favourite actor was the green-eyed muscleman Hrithik Roshan.

'Oooh Ashok, we must find ones just like Hrithik for Surya and Anjani. We must go to India and bring one for each of them!' Ma insisted that he was the only really good-looking Indian actor fit for her granddaughters.

Whenever the girls wanted a translation of the melodramatic scenes of a Bollywood movie, Ma and Nirmala shushed them without any explanations. The two older women would get so engrossed in the tragedies unfolding on screen they wanted no disturbances at all. Eventually Anjani and Surya gave up on understanding the plot and would find something else to do. Then one day, Ashok discovered the sub-title function on the DVD player and his daughters could finally partake in all the emotions evoked by Indian cinema. Anjani made a mental note to learn proper Hindi before she visited India – the motherland.

'Hello, Earth to Anjani,' said Gita, waving her hand in front of Anjani's face.

'Huh? Oh, sorry honey. I'm thinking about home again.'

Anjani sat down on her new bed. Gita quickly joined her and put a slender arm around her best friend.

'Hey, come now. Don't be sad. Remember, this is a new phase of our lives. Your mum and dad and Ma wouldn't want you moping around. And you have me, you know!' Gita's optimism always did the trick.

'I know. I just can't help it. I saw my Daddy cry for the first time today.' Saying this brought fresh tears to Anjani's face.

'I know how you feel. I had my own pity party with Mummy and Daddy at home. But I told you your father has a soft spot for you. And don't you worry, he always will. Now shake it off and drink up my friend. We have lots of exploring to do. I believe there's a first-years' welcome party at the Union this evening. I think we should be there.' Gita pushed the cold Steri Stumpie into Anjani's hand. She knew Anjani responded well to a plan of action. She was pedantic about having a purpose to every moment of her life.

'What? Gita, I'm surprised at you! Since when do you care about the party scene? Have you secretly been spending time with Surya?'

'Of course not. But this is a new place. We need to get out there and meet more people. And besides, there is someone special I want you to meet.' Gita had a naughty smile on her face.

'Wow, it hasn't even been a day yet, and you've met someone? Now I'm beginning to feel like I don't know you at all, Gita Patel.'

'No, it's not like that, silly girl. You'll see. Be ready at seven thirty. I'll pick you up after supper.'

Anjani knew she'd have to wait and see. There was no point trying to get a secret out of Gita.

Supper consisted of a piece of boiled chicken, some gigantic grains of what resembled rice, a salad made of grated carrots and pineapple, and toast. Anjani wondered if this was how non-Indian people ate. Surely food was not supposed to be this bland? It seemed like an injustice to the chicken that it had absolutely no flavouring or spice. The rice made her miss home and the fragrance of traditional basmati and flaky, hot roti. After pecking at the chicken, she ate the sweet salad and had a cup of tea with the slice of toast, hoping there would be some real food at the first-years' welcome party.

At exactly seven thirty, Gita was blaring over the intercom again. Anjani met her at the front door dressed in a pair of blue jeans, her favourite emerald green chiffon blouse and a pair of bead-embellished gold sandals. After people-watching that afternoon around campus, the girls had realised that the dress code was dress down, much to Anjani's relief. Rhodes presented a welcome change from Durban's super fashionistas. Her hair was tied back into a loose ponytail and her face was fresh with black eye-liner and mascara and a hint of pink lip-gloss.

'Wow, girlfriend! You are going to break some hearts tonight,' said Gita.

'Ha ha. Very funny. We both know you are the showstopper for the evening!' Anjani's friend didn't have to try hard before masculine attention found her, not to mention a few envious female stares.

At that moment, Anjani decided that nothing would stop her from having a good time. She took Gita's arm in hers as they sauntered off to the Students' Union. There was a fresh yet mischievous spirit in the air. For the first time since arriving at university, Anjani's mood changed. A new sense of confidence found its way into her heart. As they entered the Union building, the sound of laughter and the smell of beer mixed with old carpet assaulted Anjani's senses. A group of seniors stared at them as they walked past. They were no doubt at this party to scope out the fresh meat. Before she could realise what was happening, Gita had removed her arm from Anjani's grasp and was walking towards the guys.

'Come Anjani, I want to introduce you,' Gita was saying. She grabbed Anjani's hand and pulled her forward. 'Hi bro. Howsit going?' She was so familiar with one of them. He was tall, with gingery brown curly hair and fair skin like Gita's.

'Hey Geets.'

He was hugging her now. How could she be so easy? Or maybe she knew him from back home. It was all so confusing, but he was very handsome. His eyes turned to meet Anjani's. They were light brown and enchanting.

'Oh sorry, let me introduce you. Himal, this is my bestest friend in the whole world, Anjani. Anjani, this is my big brother, Himal.'

Anjani heard Gita's voice, but she was lost in his eyes. Himal. Is that what his name was?

'Hi Anjani. Nice to finally meet the girl I never stop hearing about from my baby sister.'

His voice was deep yet soothing. It rolled off his tongue like creamy vanilla ice cream on a hot summer's day. Was Anjani really having these thoughts? *Snap out of it. This is Gita's brother you are drooling over. How inappropriate.*

'Uh, nice to meet you too. Gita's mentioned you loads of times, but she never told me you studied here.' Anjani turned to her friend with a quizzical face.

'Well, I didn't think it meant anything to you,' retorted Gita.

'Huh, it doesn't really. It just means that we can't get up to mischief with big brother keeping a close eye on you.' Anjani thought this was a good comeback.

'Well, from what I've heard, you aren't much of a mischief-maker,' replied Himal. 'But your twin sister is.'

And there goes the conversation. Surya always managed to steal the attention, even with people she hadn't met.

'Well, perhaps I'll surprise you. It was nice meeting you. Gita, I'm going inside to get something to drink. Are you coming?' The mention of her twin sister made Anjani wonder where she was tonight. Her instinct to check on Surya kicked in and she made for the dancing crowds in front of her.

'OK, see you later, big brother.' Gita ran after her friend.

Himal watched Anjani as she walked away. He sensed that he had offended her by mentioning her twin sister. He wondered if sibling rivalry existed between them. She was beautiful in an intriguing way. He wanted to get to know her better.

RED ROSES

The twins settled into their dormitories and campus routines and relied less and less on campus maps. Lectures started and Anjani got more comfortable once she had mental stimulation, but she had to admit that embracing campus life and its associated parties and socialising provided an interesting alternative to her high-school days.

Tomorrow was Valentine's Day and for the first time in her young life, Anjani was fantasising about someone special. When she came out of a lecture hall, Himal was sitting in the sun with his friends. She had to stop herself from admiring the golden glow that the sun created around him. As soon as he saw her, he stopped talking and smiled. Anjani noticed his friends nudge each other as they realised who had caught Himal's attention.

'Hi Himal. How're you doing?' Anjani heard herself say.

'Hi. Good thanks, and you?' How many girls' hearts had he melted with that voice?

'Fine thanks, just going to another lecture. Take care.' There was no point hanging around sheepishly.

'Oh right. Me too. Sorry, these are my friends, Dave and Jay. Guys this is Anjani.' She loved the way he said her name.

'Hi. Nice to meet you.' She shook their hands. They seemed very interested in her, making her feel even more awkward. 'OK, see you around then. I've gotta go find Chem Major.' It wasn't a lie.

'Oh, let me show you where it is. I still have a few minutes. I'll catch you guys later.' Himal was walking next to Anjani before she could object.

'It's really not necessary. I'm sure I'll find it on my own. I have a map, Himal.'

'So are you saying you wouldn't like to spend more time with me?' he teased.

She laughed. 'You're funny. Well to be honest, I'm not sure your sister would be too happy that you're taking such an interest in me, you know, being her best friend and all that.' Did that sound overconfident? Maybe he was just a nice guy and he didn't really fancy her. Why would he, when he could probably have any girl on campus?

'Actually, she couldn't wait for me to meet you. I wish she had introduced me to you a lot sooner.'

Oh wow.

'And here is Chem Major. Umm. So, can I catch up with you later, Anjani?' He looked down at his shifting feet.

'Of course you can. Thanks for walking me to my lecture. What time … should I expect you?' Now Anjani was the hesitant one. This was all happening so suddenly, but she wanted to be around him. Something about him drew her in.

'After dinner, let's say around eight, if that's fine with you?'

'OK, call me on the intercom. It's Prince Alfred House.' She wanted to make sure he got to her dorm.

'I know. See you then, Anjani.'

He knew? How? Gita, of course.

For once, Anjani didn't pay much attention to the history of early hominids in her anthropology lecture. Perhaps she was infatuated with Himal and none of this was real. To her lecturer, white-haired Mr Rose, the skull of *Australopithecus* had never seemed so exciting to a student before as to this pretty Indian girl who couldn't stop smiling throughout the entire lecture.

That evening, as the clock struck 8pm, Anjani put on her kohl. It made her feel captivating. She thought of Preity Zinta, another Bollywood actress with the 'girl next door' style. Ma thought she looked exactly like Preity Zinta. If Ma was here, she would be shouting at Anjani for inviting a boy to her room. But 9pm came and went. Anjani was so nervous that at first she didn't notice the time flying by. Then it was 10pm and still no sound from the scratchy intercom.

'Face it, Anjani. You're not girlfriend material!' she said, punishing the mirror with her words.

Himal never showed up and, for the first time, Anjani cried over a boy.

–

While the girls of Prince Alfred House started Valentine's Day with a single red rose and chocolate heart at their doorsteps, Anjani soothed her tender heart and wished for Cupid's arrow to strike. Surely there were other nice guys on this campus, not just jerks who made empty promises and toyed with a girl's emotions. She would be happy if she never saw Himal on campus again. She was glad she hadn't told anyone about her feelings for him. Clearly he was having some fun at the expense of a naive little first-year.

It was student tradition at Rhodes University that on the evening of Valentine's Day, the guys from a male residence escorted the girls from a female residence to the annual Valentine's bash. This year, the boys of Piet Retief House on the hill were escorting the girls of Prince Alfred House. Eventually all the houses met for one mammoth gathering at the Great Hall.

Anjani watched as the boys filed into Prince Alfred's common room. They were all dressed in white shirts with red ties and black pants. Each of them held a single yellow rose. She had to admit it was all very gentlemanly, although some of her dorm-mates giggled as they noticed a few shaky 'gentlemen' who had started the party earlier in the afternoon with a half-jack or two of some potent alcoholic concoction.

The girls of Prince Alfred were instructed to wear pink and white. Anjani had to borrow a white skirt from her neighbour Sade as she didn't own many white pieces of clothing. She'd always found white to be such a bland colour, like a blank canvas.

After one of the subwardens introduced himself and the guys of Piet Retief House, each girl was escorted by her very own gentleman on the short journey to the Great Hall. Anjani held onto the arm of Zaheer – a stocky guy with thick hair and skin that resembled a war zone. She wondered why Cupid played such tricks on her. She decided to look past his appearance and get to know more about his personality. Unfortunately this proved challenging as Zaheer was so nervous she couldn't get more than one-word answers out of him.

Eventually, Anjani gave up and excused herself to go to the ladies' room. She stared at her reflection in the mirror and let out a huge sigh. How could a few brief encounters with Himal take over her emotions so easily? Not to mention the disappointment of his no-show.

'Well sister, better get used to it. Guys will be guys,' her reflection told her.

She decided to get a drink, hang out with her dorm friends for a bit and then go back to her room. One consolation for this Valentine's Day was that she wasn't sitting at home with her parents. At least this year was slightly different even if it wasn't romantic. As she was pouring herself some punch, a sweaty palm tapped her arm. It was Zaheer.

'Anjani, er … would you … would you like to dance?' Wow, he could actually string a sentence together.

'Can I just finish my drink, Zaheer? Thanks.' That would buy her some time to escape. Then she caught the disappointment in his eyes.

It dawned on her that if she ran out on Zaheer, she would be no better than Himal who hadn't kept his word to her. So she gulped half her punch, set the cup down and walked over to Zaheer. His face lit up when he saw her coming towards him. At least she had the pleasure of knowing she had made his day.

It was a harmless dance. Zaheer was too shy to get closer than a foot from Anjani. When the song ended, he politely thanked her for making this his first special Valentine's Day. Anjani couldn't help but be touched by his innocence. There was hope for good men out there, she thought.

She decided to call it a night and head back to her room. Prince Alfred House was close enough to the Great Hall, across a large field. The air was warm and still. It would certainly make for a romantic night for lovers all over campus. And for drunken lust-seekers too. With all the sudden freedoms of university life, she wondered how anyone ever made it to graduation.

Anjani was lost in these thoughts when she stepped into a bunch of flowers on the footpath. Red roses – how corny. She picked them up and looked for a note or card. She couldn't see a thing in the dark. She decided to take the flowers to her dorm so she could read the card and return it to its rightful owner. She got to the front door and pulled out the card.

It read, *I know these won't make up for my actions, but I can explain. I'm so sorry, Anjani. Turn around now.*

Anjani turned around to find Himal holding a puppy-dog plush toy and a heart-shaped balloon.

'Please say you'll forgive me?' His enchanting brown eyes matched the large, plastic puppy-dog eyes of the plush toy. Did he know she collected plush toys? Had he spoken to Gita about this?

'Himal. What are you doing here?' Well that was a dumb question to ask. He was asking for her forgiveness. 'I mean, what could you possibly want from me? Haven't you had your fun already? This is getting a bit old, you know. I may be a first-year, but I'm not daft.' The heat rose in her cheeks.

'OK, I know you're mad. But please let me explain. I wasn't trying to hurt you, I promise.' He sounded desperate.

'Himal, I'm tired right now. Say what you want to say and then please leave me alone.' She wasn't going to fall for his game again.

'OK, listen. Last night I was on my way here after supper. And then I got a call from Jay. You remember my friend Dave? Well, last night, someone drove into him. What's worse is that the guy who drove into him was a sloshed taxi driver. This driver insisted that it wasn't his fault and we had to call the police and get to Dave. He was threatening to hit Dave. Anyway, to cut a long story short, I had to help him out. He's been a good friend, always there for me since we got to varsity. I didn't stand you up, I just couldn't get to you in time. It was well past ten when we finished at the cop-shop. And I didn't have your number so I couldn't tell you what had happened. I was hoping to bump into you on campus today, but we didn't see each other.'

Anjani looked into his pleading eyes. He didn't sound like he had made the whole story up and she was too tired to stand outside her dorm arguing with a guy.

'Fine, you had to help your friend. I understand. No hard feelings. I'll see you around, Himal.' She opened the main door.

'No, wait! These are for you. Can't we at least talk? It's only 8:30pm and tomorrow's Saturday.' He pushed the puppy and balloon into her hands. 'Anjani … please can I make it up to you tonight?'

Alarm bells went off in her head. What did he mean make it up to her tonight? Did he think he was going to get lucky? Because of one sob story about his friend? Or was she overreacting?

Himal saw the confusion on her face. 'Sorry, that came out all wrong. I meant, would you like to go out for a coffee with me so we can chat some more? I'd … I'd really like to get to know you better. That's all. Please say yes?'

His smile was irresistible, drawing Anjani in again. 'OK, one coffee. That's it. I've had a really long day.'

He held out a hand for her.

'By the way, Happy Valentine's Day.' He whispered these words into her ear as his lips brushed her cheek, sending goosebumps down her arms. She was silent, afraid that her mouth might betray her feelings.

She looked up and smiled. Himal wanted to kiss her soft pink lips but realised she didn't fully trust him yet. He had to give her time. He believed she was special: beautiful on the outside, intelligent and good on the inside. He would have to win her heart.

That night, Anjani returned to her dorm room with a blush on her cheeks. Was this what it felt like to fall in love? One cup of coffee had turned into two cups of hot chocolate as they'd spent hours talking about her life back home with Gita, and his three years on campus and the antics he had got up to with his friends. There was something genuine about him. He didn't put up a front when he talked with her. The conversation flowed so easily.

Anjani found it fascinating that he believed in other beings and outer worlds. Most people thought she was crazy to believe in the soul of the world and synchrodestiny, but Himal listened. He admitted that he wouldn't be caught talking about such things with his buddies, but that didn't stop him from reading about it at the Esoteric Society on campus. Anjani made a note to join that society at the next Open Day. Himal was eager to introduce her to the other members.

That night, as Anjani's head hit her pillow, she thanked Cupid and all the other angels of love for bringing their two hearts together. Her mind was still suspicious of Himal's motives, but she loved his company and his gentle spirit. In her dreams, a glowing being smiled down on her. He was so breathtakingly handsome, human, yet angelic. She woke up in the early hours of the morning, certain that the being she had seen was a sign. Himal was meant to be a part of her life. She wasn't sure in what way, but she was more than willing to find out.

In the months that followed, Anjani let her emotions take charge and spent more time with Himal. Gita came to hear about these meetings. Thankfully, she didn't object.

'My best friend with my favourite brother? Why would I be upset? At least I'll know where to find the both of you!' she teased. Perhaps good-natured authenticity ran in their family.

SURYA'S HOUSE OF PARTIES

Surya was thrilled with the set up. Everything she'd envisaged for the décor and venue had materialised, down to the finest detail. She was especially pleased with the way her hair and outfit had come together.

'It was a close call but don't I look faaaabulous?' she asked in her best Scarlet O'Hara accent, in front of a gold-framed mirror. She was standing in the Victorian party parlour.

'Not too bad, actually! Pretty damn good if you ask me.' The reflection of a tall man came into view. He was astonishingly well built for an Indian guy. Surya stared at him for a moment.

'And you are?' She pulled herself together.

'Prathik Rai.'

He took her hand and kissed it with soft, warm lips that sent shivers down Surya's neck. Now this was a charmer she could get to know better.

'Does the good-looking lady have a name?'

She raised her eyebrows. 'I'm Surya. Welcome to the House of Parties. Which faculty are you from?'

'Surya? Like the Hindu Sun God, hey? Nice. No faculty. I'm visiting my cousin. He's a bit of a nerd from the computer science department. But he knew about your party. Apparently your gigs have quite a reputation on this campus. I wonder why that is?'

Surya made a mental note to meet more com-sci guys if they all had cousins like this. She thought she detected a hint of scepticism in his voice. Did he not think this was one of the best events on any campus? She had done her homework. No student had ever planned a party on this scale in the history of all Rhodes' students. The question annoyed Surya, but she relished the challenge of proving herself to him.

'I take it you haven't been out much lately. My parties are known as campus highlights. Sure, it's a challenge to outdo my previous events but I love it. And right now I have to check on my peeps, if you'll excuse me.'

She flicked back her curls and started to glide across the room. She was certain her sudden retreat from their conversation would do the trick of keeping him interested. He took her hand in his before she could move away and placed the other around her slender waist.

'It was a real pleasure to meet you, Miss Surya, goddess of light.'

She flashed a perfect smile at him. Very easy, he thought as he watched her walk away. She seemed to ooze wealth. He'd heard someone mention her name in connection with the racing-red SLK parked outside. He'd certainly take some time to check her out for a few more hours.

At 2am the party was in full swing with no sign of slowing down.

'This one's gonna go until daybreak, guys.' Surya was extremely pleased with herself as she clinked glasses with her friends.

Everyone cheered and the alcohol flowed freely. Surya and her friends were hedonistically happy. There was enough brandy and Coke in her system to keep her warm and fuzzy, but not enough to make her stagger like a drunk in her stilettos. Surya was on a high as she danced to some nineties music on the Vegas-style dance floor.

'Oh this takes me back to primary-school days! Where's my Jenny now? She needs to hear this!'

Earlier, Surya had begged Anjani to attend the party, promising the best event ever on campus. But the look Anjani had given her indicated zero interest. Lately, it seemed that all she did was spend time holed up in some Esoteric Society common room. And there seemed to be an interest in her best friend's brother. Surya hoped she would at least show up for a few minutes to support her twin. Having swayed her hips around the five dance floors searching for Anjani, Surya plonked herself on a leather couch back in the Vegas room to rest her aching feet.

'She won't hear the end of this if she doesn't come and at least meet me tonight!'

The alcohol was beginning to make Surya emotional. She had to admit that all the planning for this event, coupled with the celebration, was starting to tire her out. A warm, soft hand touched her shoulder. She looked up to meet the deep brown eyes of her twin.

'Oh Jenny, my darling. You came!' Surya's heart filled up with love as she hugged her sister.

Anjani smelt the brandy on her sister's breath as she hugged her a little too tightly. She looked as if she was about to pass out.

'Surya, hi. I'm so glad I found you. But are you OK? You seem … well … a bit drunk!'

Surya glared at Anjani, but instead of shouting at her, she burst into fits of laughter. Anjani couldn't help but join in.

'Why are you laughing, Surya?'

'Because I *am* drunk, Jenny! You're right, and I'm tired so it's hitting me even more!' Surya could hardly stand now. Anjani sensed that something wasn't right. Surya's energy was normally boundless.

'Is that all you've been doing? Drinking? Who have you been drinking with?'

'Well, yeah, just my favourites. Captain Morgan and brandy and Coke. You know my favourites. With Ash and them. You know Ash. Isn't he a darling?' Surya was slurring now.

'OK, come on, I'll take you back to your room now. I think you've had enough for tonight.'

'No, come on now, Jenny. What happened to that girl I knew in first term? She showed me a thing or two or three about partying! Come, let's dance. They were playing Vanilla Ice earlier, just for you Jenny. I can get the DJ to play it again!' Surya was pulling Anjani to the dance floor, but she was struggling to coordinate her feet, let alone her arms.

'No, no, no, Surya, we're going home. Come on.'

But before, she could speak again, Surya's long-time friend Ashraf was standing next to her.

'There you are, Su. I was wondering what happened to you. The dance floor is missing your moves. Oh, hi, Jenny, how you doing? Double trouble now!'

Ashraf was a fairly decent guy. He was Muslim, so he didn't drink alcohol, but what he didn't dabble in by way of booze, he made up for in narcotics. Anjani knew that he could score some weed whenever he needed to. She'd heard about his antics at high-school. This was the only thing that worried her when it came to Surya's friendship with him.

'Hey, Ashraf. I think Surya's had enough. She can hardly stand up straight. Forget about dancing. I think I'm gonna take her back to res.' Anjani hoped the voice of reason would work with Surya's sober friend.

'Nonsense, you must also come and enjoy the party. And I'll take you two home later. Come on, the night is still young and you're beautiful!' That had been Ashraf's favourite line for as long as Anjani could remember. He'd used it throughout their high-school lives.

'Why are you two talking about me like I'm not here?' Surya screamed. 'Anjani, if you don't want to be here, go home. I'm sick and tired of your old prude attitude. Now I want to dance and that's what I'm gonna do!' She attempted to storm off on her red high heels but only managed a stagger, leaving Anjani and Ashraf staring after her.

Anjani's irritation grew. 'That's it! I'm tired of looking out for her. She's right. When it comes to her, I end up looking like an old prude and I'm not going to do it any more. She can sleep here for all I care.' She sat down and crossed her arms. Ashraf sat down next to her.

'Hey, relax sister. I'm here with her. I know you worry about her, but she's safe on this campus and I'm never too far away. She just enjoys having a good time.' His voice was a little too relaxed for Anjani's liking, but she decided to let it go.

'You know Ashraf, I would also like to have a good time for once, without having to worry if she is overdosing on something! Why can't I enjoy myself without wondering if she is taking something to such an extreme that she needs to be physically rescued? And then the next morning, she proclaims that she's had the time of her life and nothing was wrong.'

'Aren't you exaggerating a little bit, Jenny? Overdosing? I don't think Su's ever overdosed. Sure, she goes a bit too far sometimes, but she knows her limits. Don't worry about her, I'll take her home. You can go if you want to or you can join us and have a good time. Please say you'll stay.'

Anjani had to admit that Ashraf was sweet despite his weed-induced high. But the thought of dancing after her sister's prude comment made her angry. 'No, she said I should go home, so that's what I'm going to do. But please will you look out for her? She's acting weirdly tonight.'

As she walked home, she realised that maybe it was time to break the cycle of looking out for Surya. Maybe she needed to find her own way out of the crazy situations she caused for herself. How else would she learn to take responsibility for her actions? Anjani realised that this was also a lesson for her. By not rescuing Surya at every wrong turn, she was closing a chapter in their relationship and dedicating more time to her own pursuits. She wondered what Himal was up to and couldn't help smiling to herself.

–

Surya stared into his chiselled face. In the darkness of the dance floor, he smelt fresh and his hands were so strong on her waist. He had planted warm kisses all over her neck and chest. His lips sent shivers down her back. She wanted more. She pushed up closer against him. She wanted him to feel her curves and pine for more of her. But he wasn't looking at her with desire. He seemed distracted. She wanted to say something to him so she could have his full attention. But everything around her seemed to have slowed down. She saw white light. The deafening music seemed to be coming from very far away.

–

'Where is she now?' At 3am, Ashraf was walking from dance floor to dance floor. Surya was last seen flirting with a guy in a leather jacket. They were dancing a little too closely.

'Arrgh, Jenny's not gonna like this, man.' Alarm bells were going off in Ashraf's head, but he was feeling a bit fuzzy too.

'Hey man, what are you, like her bodyguard? She can take care of herself. She organised this whole party, man,' said Ashraf's friend Marc. He was upset because Surya had run off with Mr Leather Jacket and he didn't get a chance with her.

'Yeah, guess you're right. She's one crazy chick, man. I'm sure she'll turn up eventually.' Ashraf had the munchies. 'Dude, let's go get some grub. I could eat a horse.'

–

He parked her convertible behind the cottage. In the moonlight, she lay passed out in the car, a dead weight, occasionally mumbling incoherent sentences while he organised the room keys. He dragged her into the room and bolted the door. Nobody had seen them leave the party or noticed that her car was gone. Now that she was completely unconscious, she was his to play with.

'So what do we have here? A spoilt little rich bitch out cold?' He whistled as he pulled down her skirt.

UNWELCOME REALISATIONS

Light came pouring in through the dirty window. Surya could make out a spider web in the corner. She hated spiders. It was time to clean her res room. She sat up and inhaled a pungent smell. These weren't her cotton percale sheets. This wasn't her bed.

Surya was naked and her body ached. There were blue bruises all over her upper arms. Her head throbbed and she felt wet and sore in her most private place. It took a lot of effort for her to move the stale duvet. The blood on the sheets made her gasp.

'What the fuck's happened to me?' Surya's eyes searched the strange room. She tried to get up, but it hurt too much.

'He … hello? Is anybody there?'

Panic started to set in. Where was she? And with whom? The last thing she could remember was shouting at Anjani and then dancing with Ashraf. But Ashraf would never leave her here, would he?

It was a long time before Surya could lift herself off the bed and clean up. She realised she didn't have her clothes, car keys, phone or wallet. Tears poured down her face. For the first time in her life, Surya felt total fear and abandonment. It dawned on her that not only had she been robbed of all her belongings, she had been raped too. The pain between her legs and the blood confirmed it.

Raped. Even the thought seemed unreal. She had to get out of this place. Or was it safer to hide here? Away from the rest of the world. She got into the dusty shower. She didn't care about the spiders or the cold water. She needed to clean herself. The tears that poured out of her insides mixed with the water as she rubbed her skin vigorously until her arms ached even more than before. The running water drowned her screaming agony.

ANJANI'S MISSING A TWIN

The neon red digits of her alarm clock said 08:00 when Anjani woke from a restless sleep. She had been angry with Surya as she'd slumped into bed last night and she still felt upset even though it was a bright, beautiful morning. It was unlike her to feel so emotional after a fight with her sister. Normally she got over it pretty quickly, but this morning she couldn't understand her deep sense of unease. She decided to get dressed and find her twin. No doubt Surya would be hung-over and irritable but Anjani didn't care as long as she got to say her piece.

It was almost nine before she was able to appease her hunger with a bowl of oats. A male voice called her name over the scratchy intercom.

'Jenny, are you there man? I mean, Anjani, hello?' It was Surya's sidekick, Ashraf.

'Hey Ashraf. Hang on a sec. I'm coming upstairs.' Anjani unwillingly abandoned her growling tummy along with her bowl of oats. What did he want?

'Hi, Jenny. Sorry to barge in on you so early. But, er, I need to ask you something.' Ashraf mumbled his last sentence and looked at Anjani hesitantly.

'What's up, Ashraf?'

'Well, I was wondering, er … have you, er … Have you seen Su this morning?' Ashraf could barely get his words out. Anjani began to wonder why. Did Surya get into trouble yet again?

'No, I was having breakfast before going over to her dorm.'

'Well, then I think we … Anjani, we have a problem. She's not at her dorm room. I've just come from there.'

'What? What do you mean she's not there? She's probably still sleeping and doesn't want to answer the intercom. Don't worry, I'll go wake her up.' Anjani was now even more irritated with her sister.

'No, Jenny, you don't understand man. I was, well, I checked her room. I was there the whole night. You see, I lost my room key, but I had … I had her key. So … so I crashed in her room, and I thought she would, you know, I thought she would show up later and kick me out or let me crash on the floor or something. But dude, she didn't even come home.'

Irritation turned into fear and the deep-seated unease from earlier came back. As crazy as Surya was, she always let somebody know where she was going to be for the night. Anjani checked her phone. There were no messages or calls from Surya.

'Ashraf, come with me. We're going to go wait for her back at her room.' She was out the front door before Ashraf could say another word.

By 11am, Anjani was pacing Surya's room. It smelt stale, like cigarette smoke. Probably from Ashraf spending the night.

'OK, let's face it – she's not coming back here. We need to retrace her activities from last night. Ashraf, when last did you see her and where?'

Anjani had rescued her sister a million times. She knew what had to be done, but this time she was more anxious than ever before. Perhaps it was because she didn't have to explain anything to anyone. Her parents weren't on campus, so there was nobody to reprimand Surya for her irresponsible actions, nobody to ground her for bad behaviour. Surya was free to misbehave and that's exactly what she had done. Anjani was trying to fill her head with these thoughts. She didn't want to face the possibility that something had happened to her sister.

'Well, at about half two she didn't want to hang around with us. She had met up with this guy. I don't remember her telling me his name. She said she would catch up with me later. She was pretty wasted by then so I didn't want to leave her there with him. But she started shouting at me and he became defensive. He was a big dude and I didn't want to cause a scene so I let her dance with him.' Ashraf was still mumbling.

'OK, fine. So she was dancing with a guy. That's typical Surya behaviour. And then? What did the guy look like?' Anjani sensed that Ashraf was feeling harassed but she didn't care.

'Listen, Jenny. I'm sorry man. I know I said I'd take her home, but she started overreacting. She insisted she wanted to dance with this guy on her own. So I let her dance with him while I was, well, you know, having a smoke. I must have gone to the shanks or something like ten minutes later. When I got back, they were gone.'

'What do you mean gone? Where did they go? And you still haven't told me what this guy looked like, Ashraf.' Anjani was losing her patience. If Ashraf was high, he could've missed important details.

'OK, OK, chill man. I don't know where they went, but another friend of ours, Skates, was keeping an eye for me when

I went to the gents. He said, er, he said that that guy had his arm around Su and they had walked out together. They were looking real cosy, if you know what I mean. Oh, yeah and the guy, well, I don't really remember his face, but he was tall and pretty big built. He was Indian I think and he had a leather jacket on. Oh yeah, and blue jeans. When he looked at me when I was trying to talk to Su, he looked pretty hectic man, like he would fix my face if I came any closer. That's why I was worried about her. And that's why I was hoping she had come to you.' Ashraf's voice lowered as he said the last few words.

'Oh, God. What are we going to do? This is serious. She could be anywhere by now. What if … what if he's done something to her?' Anjani fell into a heap on Surya's bed. Her worst fears were being confirmed by Ashraf's story. 'We need to go look for her. We need to turn this campus upside down. Someone's bound to have seen her.' She had to pull herself together until she found Surya.

'Er, sorry Jenny? I need to go back to my dorm now. I'm seriously suffering here. I'll join you later. Sorry, dude. I've gotta go.' Ashraf was walking out the door.

'No, Ashraf. You will stay here in case she comes back.' Anjani grabbed Surya's wasted friend and shoved him on Surya's bed. 'You're not going to leave this room, you hear me?'

What kind of friend was Ashraf to have left his closest child-hood buddy with a complete stranger? Smoking dope seemed more important to him than friendship. Anjani tried to hold back her tears. How could she have left her sister with such fools? 'The responsible one' should have known better. As she walked out the main entrance to Surya's residence, she bumped into someone. Her eyes were clouded by tears until she wiped her face. She looked up into familiar brown eyes – Himal.

'Anjani! Hey, what's wrong?'

She wanted to fall into his arms and cry her eyes out on his warm chest, but something stopped her. 'Himal, I have to find Surya. She didn't come home last night and nobody knows where she went after her party.' She fought more tears as she spoke. 'I have to go now.'

He grabbed her arm. 'Hang on. Anjani, you don't look like you should be doing this on your own. Let me help you.'

'Oh no, you don't have to do that. I'm sure you have better things to do with your time than chase someone's wayward sister. This might take me a long time, anyway.' She didn't want any distractions.

'I'm not doing anything important, Anjani. Let me help you. I want to, and besides, I know this campus better than you do.' He had a good point there. Perhaps that would speed up the search. 'Now tell me, where did you last see Surya?'

'She was at that House of Parties gig of hers until about half past two this morning. I left her after we argued. She'd had too much to drink and I wanted her to come home with me. But she told me to leave her alone and I got angry with her. So I left. She was with her old friend Ashraf who was too busy getting high to notice her leaving with some stranger.' Anjani was out of breath and in tears at the end of the story.

Himal put an arm around her. He didn't say anything, just held her as she cried. He let her finish before wiping her face with his fingers.

'Anjani, listen to me. I'll help you look around this campus. But we have to be prepared for the fact that Surya might not even be here any more. This guy she was with. Did you see him?'

'All I know is that he was a tall, well-built guy in a leather jacket and blue jeans. And he might have been Indian. Oh God, that sounds like such a pathetic description. But that's all I could get out of Surya's wasted friend.'

'OK, Anjani, you might not like the sound of this, but it is a reality. This guy might have taken your sister to a hideout on campus so they could do more than dance, if you know what I mean. I'm sorry to say it.'

She wondered how naive he thought she was. Most teenagers had already lost their virginity in high-school. But he was right. She had to accept that Surya might have wanted to part with her virginity at her party. Surya refused to accept the Hindu tradition of abstinence from sex before marriage. She had told Anjani that she intended to explore her sexuality when they got to university.

'Himal, I get it. It's not only guys who think about getting laid. Now take me to these hideaways.' Anjani grabbed onto his arm and he led her to the hill on the upper end of campus to start their search.

—

The sun was losing its intensity. It was getting late and Anjani was tired. She hadn't had anything to eat since a bite of oats that morning. Surya was nowhere to be found. Even Himal's optimism was waning. Anjani was beginning to think that maybe Surya was not on campus and that the mysterious stranger had kidnapped her. She wondered what she was going to tell her parents and Ma. How would they handle the news of their missing child?

'There is one more place that we can look. But I've never

been there so I need to call a friend for directions.' Himal didn't wait for an answer from Anjani. He was already on the phone.

Anjani stood in the garden of Rhodes University's oldest guesthouse, watching as this gentle guy spoke into his phone. She was so grateful for all his help, even if he probably had his own motives. She couldn't have searched the entire campus on her own. It would have taken her days to find all these nooks and hideouts.

'OK, come. Let's get going.' Himal grabbed Anjani's hand once more and they ran down a side street.

A saving grace for Anjani's tired feet was that they were running downhill. They were now on the outskirts of town. The highway going back to KZN was in full view ahead of them. On the left were the plastic, compacted, mud-and-zinc roofs of the sprawling township shacks. On their right was a sign for a resort called Water's Edge. Nearby was a derelict grouping of wooden chalets overgrown by oak trees and ivy. Himal and Anjani entered what seemed like the reception building. A stocky man as old as the oak trees, with skin to match, peered at them from under his glasses.

'I take it you two want a room?'

'Er, no sir. We were wondering if you could help us. We're looking for this girl. She may have been here early this morning with a taller gentleman in a leather jacket?' Himal was ever so polite as he showed the old man Surya's photograph.

'Well, I wouldn't know about that. My maid was working the wee hours of this morning. But she only gets in at 10pm tonight. You are welcome to book a room while you wait for her?' The old man had a one-track mind.

'No, thank you.'

All they could do now was wait until 10pm to ask the maid to check Surya's photo. They walked out of the dingy reception. Anjani was overcome with tiredness and despair. They had searched everywhere but there was no sign of Surya. Himal offered to take her out for pizza. She needed to eat and they had hours to go before they could follow their only lead.

DESPAIR

The sun was starting to set. Surya had drifted in and out of consciousness. She was wrapped in the only piece of material she could find – the dirty bed sheet. She had screamed and cried herself into a state of numbness. Several times she had tried to leave the spider-infested room, but she was locked in. She had banged on the wooden door until her hands bled from the rusty nails that jutted out.

The windows were sealed shut with thick metal mesh so she couldn't break the glass to get out. Occasionally, she thought she heard movement outside the door and screamed, but nobody responded. She was convinced that she had been left to die in here. But she knew she had to keep trying to get help until she ran out of breath. With all her aches and internal pain, Surya banged on the door again. This time, she used the soiled sheet as protection for her sore hands.

Anjani returned to Water's Edge despite Himal's protest about her not eating enough. She needed to stay close to her only hope of finding Surya. Himal's friend Dave was kind enough to lend them his car, since it was late to be walking around town. They parked in front of the old oak trees a little way away from the main reception. They didn't want to be badgered by the old man again.

'Thank you Himal, for all that you've done today. I don't know why you offered to help me, but I really appreciate it.' Her words were awkward but she meant them.

'Don't thank me. We haven't made much progress. And I did it because I couldn't bear seeing you so distraught. Anjani, I know this is not the time or place, but I helped you … well, I'm here … because I care about you.'

He managed to get a smile out of her. It was a weak smile, but sincere. Then their moment was shattered by a muffled sound.

'Did you hear that?' Anjani held her breath. She waited to hear the sound again. There was nothing.

She got out the car and walked towards the wooden chalets. She sensed that she was about to find something. Something she was afraid to find. It came again – a scream. From a woman. Anjani ran to the last chalet, the one closest to the highway. The screams were dying down, but they were definitely coming from the last chalet. Himal followed her. The door was bolted on the outside. That was strange, unless someone didn't want whoever was inside to leave. She looked around to see if anyone was watching her.

'Hello, is someone in there? Are you OK?' She tried to speak up, but fear of what she might discover kept her voice low.

She banged on the door and thought about undoing the outer bolt. She jumped back as the muffled screaming started up again and someone banged at the door from the inside. Himal grabbed her shoulders and moved her aside before unbolting the door. He slowly pushed it open.

Surya lay on the floor. There was blood all over her face

and her hair was wet. Her face was streaked black from her bloodshot, mascara-stained eyes. Her shoulders and arms were bruised deep blue. Anjani almost stopped breathing, but she went straight to her sister. They had found her. That was all that mattered.

A MATTER OF FACTS

Anjani took Surya to the Health Centre on campus, knowing she'd prefer its privacy to the scale of a major hospital. She'd seen the Centre's posters on the bathroom doors at res – it was fully equipped for emergencies .

Sister Susan Johannes handed her a white pill and some water. She saw the Sister's lips moving but her voice seemed far away.

'Take this tablet. You're in shock. I need you to be strong for when Officer Jansen arrives my dear.'

Anjani wanted to say that Surya was the one who was in shock, but she obeyed the Sister.

Surya was with a doctor who'd been called in to examine her and take samples of her blood and any evidence that may have been left behind. Anjani reluctantly waited outside for the doctor to return her distraught twin. She slumped on the floor with her head between her hands. Thoughts of what she was going to do next and how she was supposed to tell her parents what had happened swam through her aching mind.

A pair of black boots screaming to be polished came into view on the gleaming cream floor.

'Ms Harsingh, I'm Warrant Officer Jansen.' He held out a hand to help her up. 'I'm sorry to hear that your sister has been through a difficult situation last night.'

'Is that what you call rape these days?' Anjani felt the heat rise in her face. Her legs were threatening to give way.

'Ma'am, until we have all the evidence, we cannot make any assumptions.' He took out a pen and clipboard. The edges of the clipboard were bent and the layers of cardboard could be seen as it expanded; a reminder of how under-resourced South Africa's police service was.

'Can you tell me your account of what happened with your sister? Then I will take her statement when she is finished with the doctor.'

Anjani thought it best to cooperate with the warrant officer. He was, after all, just being impartial and following police procedure. Her body ached with exhaustion as she recounted Ashraf's idiotic babbling, finding real help from Himal, searching all over campus, ending up at Water's Edge and hearing the faint moaning that brought them to Surya. She shivered when she remembered her sister's deathly face and the dried blood on her bruised body.

Warrant Officer Jansen watched the young lady as she was called in to speak to Dr Margot. The victim was lucky to have a sister close by. From her statement, it seemed they had a lot to process.

Sister Johannes emerged from the examination room. She nodded her head in agreement about the post-exposure prophylaxis treatment prescribed by the doctor for the victim in case she may have contracted HIV through the rape.

'Can I get the victim's statement now, Susan?' Warrant Jansen did not want to hang around the Health Centre for too long.

'I'm afraid you won't be able to Brian. She's not speaking a word at the moment. She's in terrible shock and we've treated her with some sedatives. We should get the test results tomorrow afternoon. But you can open your case in the meantime.'

'I can only open a case of theft for the stolen vehicle and the victim's belongings. You know this Susan. She has to report the sexual assault before we can investigate further.'

'Yes, but surely, with her sister's statement you can start your investigation?' Sister Johannes did not want a scandal on her hands if the police did nothing.

'My hands are tied until the victim comes forward. Let's hope she starts talking soon.'

'Let's hope so. I'll see you at church Brian.' It was best to let the policeman be. She would talk to the girl and make sure the crime got reported even if they went through the Counselling Centre or Legal Resources.

A SEARCH FOR COMFORT

It had been three days since Anjani and Himal found Surya. Anjani stayed at the Health Centre with her sister, refusing to leave Surya's side. Himal decided it was best to give the sisters their space. He only came in once a day to check on them. Gita had come too. She was worried about her best friend.

Sister Johanna had given Surya some strong painkillers. Ever since Himal and Anjani had found her, she hadn't even been able to string a sentence together. She was deeply disorientated and needed time to heal physically before her mental recovery could begin. Sister Johanna confirmed Anjani's suspicion that Surya had been raped. Anjani was overcome with grief but she had to be strong for her sister. She hadn't figured out what to say to her parents. When they called, she pretended that all was well and they'd had a great weekend. She made the excuse that Surya was out planning her next event, so she couldn't speak to them. Anjani wished with all her heart that this excuse were true and that she didn't have to see Surya in so much pain. She called upon the healing powers of the Archangels to pour their love and protection over Surya. She needed it more than ever.

Surya slept through most of the first two days, but on the

third she was awake. She sat in silence. A counselling psychologist, Dr Brown, came to see her in the morning. He recommended further rest and a supportive environment for Surya over the next few months. Anjani still hadn't said anything to their parents. She knew that time was running out before they would want to speak to Surya themselves. She had to make her well again but she'd been through too much. It was close to impossible to get her to shift focus and move forward as a survivor in such a short space of time.

Anjani considered hypnosis, but she knew from her psychology classes that the first step to recovery from any trauma is acknowledging the events that have occurred, and then working through all of the emotions stirred up by those events, before acceptance and closure could be achieved. Surya needed more time and more sessions with a professional therapist.

A week after the rape, Surya began talking again. She didn't say much, but the fact that she spoke to other people was considered progress. Two weeks later, Anjani still kept a close vigil on her twin. Sometimes, she found her in her room, crying in a corner. In these moments, Anjani would go to her and hold her tight until Surya stopped crying. As with any trauma over the course of their lives, Anjani was the only one who could calm Surya down.

Her mind flashed back to that night in the dusty old cottage every time she found Surya huddled into a corner of their room. She had convinced the dean of residences to let them move into a double room so that she could be close to her sister at night. She told her parents that they were missing each other and wanted to stay together, but she sensed they did not entirely believe her.

The hardest thing for Surya to deal with was her lack of memory of the events of that night. Blood tests had confirmed that she'd had the date-rape drug, Rohypnol, in her system. They had caught a trace of the drug just before it became unde-tectable. This also explained the gap in her memory. Anjani was certain that Surya spent hours trying to remember, but the memory of being locked up in that hole of a cabin only brought back her anxiety and fear.

Surya had dark rings around her eyes. She was only just beginning to sleep through the nights. She'd stopped attending lectures. Anjani made a mental note to speak to Surya's lecturers regarding her recovery and getting her notes for all the classes she had missed.

But Nirmala had already realised that something was wrong.

'Where is she, Anjani? I want to speak to her. Put her on the phone. What has she gone and done now?'

Anjani took in a deep breath. *Here we go again.* She hated lying to her mother.

'Mummy I told you, I don't know why she hasn't called you, but she's pretty busy with lectures and stuff.'

'Anjani Harsingh! How dare you lie to me? You have never lied to me before. I knew sending you two to varsity so far away was a terrible idea. Now if you don't tell me what is going on, I am going to come down there and see for myself what that child is up to!' Anjani had to hold the phone away from her ear.

There was no use covering it up any more; she had to tell her parents everything. And they would understand once they heard what Surya had been through.

'OK, OK. Calm down, Mum. Are you sitting down? I have some awful news to share with you. Put the phone on speaker so Daddy can also hear me.' Anjani wondered where to begin. This was the hardest thing that she'd ever had to tell her parents. She heard the crackling sounds of hot oil on the stove as her mother put on the speakerphone; probably Nanima frying samoosas for tea.

'Mum, Daddy, Surya was ... something really bad happened to Surya. She was ... she was ... kidnapped. And raped. But we found her and she is in recovery. It's really hard for her. You see, she was drugged at her party. We don't know who did this to her. Daddy, she is in a bad way. They stole all of her things. Even her car. We cancelled her bank and SIM cards and reported the car stolen. But we haven't heard anything from the police.' Anjani stopped to try and swallow the lump in her throat.

'I'm sorry I didn't say anything sooner. Mummy, I'm sorry I lied to you, but I didn't know how to tell you and I have been so busy trying to take care of Surya. She really needs me. The university is providing counselling for her, but I moved in with her because she doesn't sleep well. She cries a lot. I'm sorry; I'm doing the best I can.' Anjani's voice trailed off as it became shaky, but she was glad that she didn't have to keep the horror of that night to herself any more.

There was silence on the other end of the line for a long time.

'It's OK, my child. We are coming.' Her father's reassuring voice calmed her down.

She explained the events of the party and the next day, and how she had found Surya in that wretched cabin. She could hear her mother in the background, probably telling Nanima what had happened.

As Nirmala climbed into bed that night, she found that she couldn't sleep. Images haunted her: Surya in a dirty cabin; a man taking away her innocence; Surya lying unconscious. It was all too much to take in. Surely this wasn't real. Anjani had a vivid imagination; perhaps this was all a story she was spinning to get them to come visit. That must be it.

But what if it wasn't a story? How could she face her daughters? Nirmala almost felt responsible for the rape. She should have insisted that the girls study at home. As soon as she had let her guard down and allowed them to leave her protection, they got hurt. Scarred for life, in Surya's case. Who would marry her now? What would Nirmala say to the community and their family?

She thought about what a treacherous world this had become. It was a curse to be born a woman in this country. Everywhere you turned, a woman was a victim of abuse or rape or murder. Nirmala thought about her karma and her past lives. Was this her bad karma catching up with her? That's what all the neighbours and family members would say. Perhaps they didn't have to find out. Maybe it was a good thing this hadn't happened here in Durban.

As she closed her eyes, Nirmala decided it would be best to leave the girls at Rhodes University. They would be away from the prying eyes of this Indian community. The Harsingh family name would not be shamed. Surya had done a lot to disgrace the family in the past with all her high-school antics and nonsense she got up to with boys. Nirmala wondered what her cheeky daughter had done to be singled out as the one that rapist chose. Surya had gone too far this time. So far that she has harmed herself forever. Nirmala didn't know how she was going to clean up this mess. Her thoughts faded into black as sleep finally came.

–

For the second time in his life, Ashok was close to tears over one of his daughters on this campus. He had tried hard not to cry when he had said his goodbyes to Anjani at the beginning of the year, but to see Surya huddled up on her bed – her face and eyes red and sunken from all her anguish – was unbearable. She looked so much older and had dark circles around her eyes. Her skin was ashen and she appeared malnourished. She probably hadn't eaten much since this had happened. He held her as she murmured softly, although he couldn't make out what she was saying. She clung on tightly and her bony fingers dug into his arms.

At first, she'd frozen when he'd approached her bed. Then she'd looked into his eyes and known he meant no harm. Anger rose up in his chest. He wanted to kill the man who'd done this to his precious daughter. He wanted the bastard to suffer through slow torture. But first he had to see what progress the police had made.

Nirmala stood at the edge of Surya's bed. She watched as her husband comforted his daughter. She needed Surya to tell her what had happened. She needed reassurance that Surya had not brought this on herself. Her emotions confused her. She wanted to reach out to her daughter, her child, but she was angry with her. She must have provoked the rapist. Her thoughts went back to ways to cover up this mess without the whole community finding out about it.

Mrs Naidoo, the community gossip broadcaster and their neighbour, was her usual nosy self this morning as they'd left for the airport. She'd wanted to know why their sudden visit to the girls had come up. Nirmala was sure she'd picked up on their worry. Surely there was no way anyone could find out why they rushed off to the Eastern Cape. Ashok stood up to make room for Nirmala.

'Surya, I'm so sorry my child.' Nirmala hugged her daughter but her words sounded superficial. She couldn't help feeling awkward.

Anjani entered with books in her hand. She looked at her parents' worried faces. She was glad she wasn't on her own any more. Tears welled up in her eyes as she hugged her father. Her mother was holding Surya's hand, but Surya was silent. She was hugging her knees to her chest. Nirmala smiled meekly at Anjani and turned her attention back to her first daughter.

'Surya, I know you are in shock, but I have to ask you how this all happened.'

Anjani couldn't believe her ears. 'Mummy, not now!'

'No Anjani, I have to know. We left home in such a hurry and we have to go back soon. What will we tell the family, Nanima, the neighbours? The way Mrs Naidoo was looking through her kitchen window at us.'

'Who cares about Mrs Naidoo? Why do you have to tell them anything? This is our family crisis and it should stay with our family. You don't have to say anything!' How could her mother be thinking about the neighbours at a time like this? Surya needed her mother's comfort more than anything else. Not an inquisition.

'And since when have you backchatted me, huh? You think now that you going to varsity you can talk to me like that? Is this what you think? Too grown up you are now!' Nirmala was irritated. Anjani had never disrespected her before. She knew that sending her daughters to university away from home was a big mistake. This incident confirmed it. She looked at Surya. She needed to hear the whole story so she could think about what to say when she went back home.

'Surya, tell me everything. Where were you? How did you land up in that place? Who were you with? And how were you dressed up?'

Anjani exploded inside. She couldn't stand this a moment longer. Surely her mother didn't believe that the way Surya dressed had anything to do with the rape? That was such ignorant thinking but so typical of the older generation. They believed the myth that rapists look for women who are scantily clad and her mother wanted to believe the worst.

'There were hundreds of girls dressed in almost nothing that night. Not Surya. Why are you doing this to her? This is ridiculous. She's been through enough already. Can't you see she wants to move on? Why can't you just be a mother to her? I told you what happened. What, don't you believe me, now?' Anjani looked at her father for some support. Perhaps he would be the voice of reason here.

'What are you her mouthpiece now? Do you also think for her? I am her mother, not you, my dear Anjani! And why should I believe you? You lied to us. You kept this whole thing a secret for how long?' Nirmala stood to face her younger daughter. Her hands were on her hips and she was waving a finger in Anjani's face. 'It looks like you've become too big for your boots, like Surya used to be. And Surya, well, God only knows what will happen to her. But I am sure she had her part to play in this mess. She must have provoked that man who did this to her and now look how she is. And you think I'm going to sit here and listen to you barking orders at me? If I had my way, you two would have never come here! Your mouth is too big now. Hmm.'

'That's enough! From both of you.' Ashok's voice boomed across the room. He hated seeing his family torn apart. 'Nirmala, we are leaving. Now! And Anjani, we'll talk again when you two have cooled down.' He led his wife out despite her protesting looks.

As they closed the door behind them, Anjani sat on her bed in a heap. She'd really believed her mother would be more understanding of the situation. Surya needed comfort, not to be told that the whole thing was her fault. Perhaps their mother was the one who should have counselling. Anjani thought she'd suggest it to her father the next time she saw her parents.

All the while, Surya held her knees to her chest and didn't say a word. Anjani sat next to her. A tear fell down Surya's cheek. Anjani put her arm around her twin's back.

'I'm sorry you had to deal with that. You know how Mummy is. She's always so worried about what everyone else will think.' As Anjani said the words, her irritation rose. But Surya needed support. That was all that mattered.

Surya didn't speak. She thought about her mother's words. Perhaps Nirmala was right: maybe she had said or done something to provoke her rapist. Maybe that was why he'd picked her.

–

The passageway was dark. Surya breathed heavily as if she had been running for a long time. There was just enough light to make out the many doors, but all of them were shut. Except for one. The purple light of the evening sky reflected off the brown wood of that open door. She ran in and shut the door behind her.

Inside the room stood tables covered in dishevelled newspaper. In the centre of the room stood a table with a wooden box. A brass lamp was burning out. The smell of burning oil on a cotton wick rushed up Surya's nostrils. Then she saw the box of matches with the familiar red lion on its cover. Quickly she pulled at the base of the wick. She reached for a match and struck the box. The little yellow flame came to life just as she heard screaming.

Footsteps hurried closer to the door. She had shut it, but it wasn't locked. Fear tore at her insides. She reached for the bolt. The screams got louder. It was Mummy. Why was she screaming like that? She was so angry. The door slammed into Surya's shoulder. She shoved it back but not before catching a glimpse of her mother. She appeared possessed. Her normally neat hair was wild. Her eyes were beady and filled with rage. Her mouth curled into a terrifying scream. She was a devil-woman.

Surya's eyes opened with a start. She searched around the room. Anjani breathed deeply as she slept in the next bed. It was just a dream.

DAMAGED GOODS

His peacock feather quill shone as it touched the sacred page of
his eternal scroll. A smile broadened his golden elephant trunk.

The super soul was preparing to do great things with its
earthly existence. But first he must make sure that the soul was
welcomed. A message must be delivered so that destiny could be
fulfilled. There would surely be some resistance from this family, yet there was wisdom and understanding within their souls.

Ganeshji watched a prayer being offered to him. It was pure
and unselfishly offered for a sister's protection. This old soul
would be strong through the conflict that was about to unfold.
But what about her own karma?

'Matha, I need your wisdom,' he called out to Parvathi.

'What is it, Putr?' She placed her hand on his shoulder once
more.

'I'm worried about this soul. She has been bonded to her sister in this life yet she is wise and offers protection from their
previous bonds. Her path to us is almost flawless. What if the
conflict in this life tarnishes her karma?' Ganeshji's quill was
back in the ink to complete his writing.

'You worry needlessly, Putr. Observe her soul's energy as she prays to you, Sri Avighna. She understands your love for all. She may simply need reminding that the suffering inflicted on her earthly sister is not God-made. It is of human conception and action, but it too shall pass from the cycle of suffering into joy. She has ShivShakti – inner strength beyond her own comprehension. They will all find ways to fulfil the entry of the super soul. The change is inevitable but it is also complete.' Mother Parvathi smiled at the soul called Anjani.

'Of course you are right, Matha. Om Namah Shivaya.' He blessed the prayer being offered to him and his parents.

'Mushakaji, please send this message to Lord Varuna at once.' His elephant trunk uncurled, proffering a note tied with red string and gold bells. 'He'll know what to reveal.'

–

The next day Anjani met with her parents. She apologised to her mother for talking out of turn, more to keep the peace than because she was sorry.

Nirmala made Anjani repeat the nightmare story of finding Surya after the rape until she was satisfied that she had heard every detail. Anjani explained the need to be cautious around Surya as Dr Brown had suggested. She told her parents that Surya hadn't spoken a word for a week after the trauma and that too much pressure might send her back into that wordless space. She insisted that her parents meet Dr Brown before going home. Perhaps he could explain Surya's state better than she could.

'What did I do to deserve this, Ashok?' Nirmala complained back at their hotel. 'I have only ever tried to raise these girls the right way so they grow up like good girls. What I did wrong?'

She was lying on the hotel bed, her head throbbing.

They had just come back from a meeting with Dr Brown. Nirmala didn't want to hear him talk about her daughter as the victim. She was convinced that Surya had provoked her rapist. She was only too aware of Surya's promiscuous behaviour in high school. Surya was not a victim in any of those other situations. She was usually the cause of all the trouble and this time she had hurt her reputation and the family name. Nirmala imagined Ma's face as she spoke into the telephone receiver.

'Arre Bhagwan, who'll marry her now? She is spoilt. Destroyed goods. No nice family in this community will perform Khanya-dhan for this child.'

Ma was right. No family would perform the marriage ceremony and welcome Surya as their own daughter because she was now considered impure.

'It's nobody's fault, Nirmala,' Ashok insisted. 'Well at least not your fault or Surya's fault. Didn't you hear what that psychologist was saying? Rape happens everywhere and a rapist chooses his victims carefully. The bastard drugged Surya to make it easy to kidnap her. And it wasn't just about her being raped. It was a robbery too. Her car and belongings were all stolen. If I was hijacked, would you say that I did something wrong? This is South Africa. Crime is high. I just can't believe this happened to our child but we have to be strong for her. She needs us now.' His heart felt heavy with rage thinking about a man touching his daughter against her will, but this was harder for his wife to comprehend.

'Should we take the girls home now? I told you this wasn't a good idea to let them come here.' Although the damage had already been done. If only her husband had listened to her instead of his daughters. Sometimes she wondered if he loved them more than he loved her.

'If we do that, they will lose a whole year of studies. Maybe it's best to leave them to finish the year. Then we can move them back home and they can go to Natal University. Too much commotion has already happened this year.' It pained Ashok to leave his daughters here, but he knew it was time for them to deal with their lives in their own ways. 'We'll do everything we can to make things easier while they are not with us. Then we can take them home.'

Nirmala turned onto her side. She wondered if it was a good idea to bring them back home. They had both defied her and she was so angry. In a matter of a few months, they had become women of their own ways. She felt that she didn't know either of them any more. One of her biggest fears for her daughters had come true and she would be the laughing stock of the neighbourhood. How could she show her face in public when everyone heard that her daughters went away for a few months and ruined their futures? A thought suddenly struck Nirmala and she sat up.

'What if Surya contracted a disease from this? You hear in the news that men are raping virgins to cure themselves of AIDS. What if Surya is now diseased, Ashok?'

'Calm down. I checked the nurse's report. Surya was drugged but she tested negative for HIV. I think they'll repeat the test in six months, but we have to think positive for her sake. Whatever the outcome, we have to deal with it as a family. She is still our child.'

There was another issue that played on Ashok's mind but he didn't dare mention it to his wife.

ANOTHER UNWANTED REALISATION

Books lay everywhere. Surya had a lot of catching up to do. She had missed weeks of lectures and tutorials. Given her circumstances, the dean had allowed her to continue classes and catch up on those she'd missed, but everything was so confusing. There was a huge gap that Surya was trying to fill.

The memories were plaguing her again. Remembering waking up in that musty cabin became a little less painful with each passing day but it still stopped Surya every time.

A sudden wave of bile built up at the back of her throat. She tasted her breakfast gone acidic and took a sip from her water glass. That reaction had never happened before. She set the glass down and caught sight of the desk calendar. A few weeks ago time had been blurred and she hadn't known what day or month it was. Dr Brown had been helpful in getting her to come to terms with life after rape.

Now it was the end of October. In less than a month, everyone would be writing exams. Surya hoped to scrape through; anything more would be a miracle.

'October ... October?' She said it out loud as she flipped the calendar back to September. There were no dates circled in red.

Did Anjani forget? She couldn't have. She never forgot to mark their monthly cycle.

Surya flipped the calendar back to August. Anjani had circled the twentieth with an 'A' next to it to mark her period. There was no date for Surya.

She flipped back to July. There was only one red circle, on the twenty-first, with an 'A'. What were her dates?

'Oh, no. Please God, not that!' She pressed her temples with fingers that felt bonier than before. She tried to recall if the sisters at the Health Centre had given her a course of morning-after and PEP pills to take after the rape. Yes … yes … it rang a bell at the back of her mind. But there had been so many pills to take that she couldn't recall what each one treated.

Surya sank into her chair. Searching her brain for a memory of a period made her head hurt even more. It was like trying to remember the blanks on the day of the rape – pointless. The thought of a baby growing inside her was unimaginable. It would be *his* baby. She didn't even know who he was.

When Anjani returned the room was dark. The windows were still open and a cold wind was blowing the curtains. She was tired and hungry from a long day of lectures followed by tutorials. A good shower would do the trick. Had Surya gone off to the dining hall already? If that was the case, her old sister was coming back to her. She flicked the light switch and went to draw the curtains.

Surya was crouched on a corner of the bed. Her eyes were red and puffy as she squinted into the light and buried her head in her knees.

'Surya. What's wrong?' Anjani sat next to her. Her heart rebelled at the thought of calming Surya down again. If she had to admit anything to herself, it would be that she was tired of this scene. She'd thought Surya was making good progress in overcoming the rape. This showed otherwise. Surya grabbed Anjani's arms tightly and shook her.

'Did I have it, Anjani? Did you forget to mark the calendar? When was my last period, Jenny?' Her voice was soft but scratchy; she must have been crying for hours.

Anjani's mind raced as she grabbed the calendar. Their periods were always in sync, but so much had happened over the last few weeks she couldn't remember if she had marked the calendar. September was blank, but she remembered having her period because of her irritation at not finding her favourite chocolate bar at the cafeteria. And then her monthly flow had arrived between her lectures. But what about Surya? She was so busy managing Surya's emotional state that she had forgotten to ask about her period.

'I had mine on the twentieth. You should have had yours around the same time. I did forget to circle the calendar, but I'm sure I had mine.' She took Surya's hand. 'I'm sorry. I was so preoccupied with helping you heal. Can you remember if you had yours last month?'

Surya looked at her, searching for answers in her face.

'I ... I don't know. I don't know when!' Surya's voice turned into a mumble. Then it stopped short. 'Jenny, three months! Three months! What if I'm ... what if I'm pregnant? I'll kill myself. I will. I'll kill myself. I can't live with that!'

There was nothing Anjani could say to make her sister feel better. She sat there with Surya in her arms as she poured out all the tears left in her body. What had brought such unfortunate events into their lives? What had Surya done in a past life to be dealt such difficult times in this one?

An hour passed by. Surya quietened down. Anjani convinced her to eat a packet of two-minute noodles before taking a sedative. This felt all too familiar. She tucked her sister in, promising to be by her side no matter what. But how could she help if she was indeed pregnant? They were barely adults themselves. A few months ago they were hanging out in the school playground. And how would she break the news to her parents and Nanima?

Hang in there, she told herself. First they'd have to find out if Surya was really pregnant. Her thoughts were interrupted by her phone vibrating on the desk. It was an SMS from Himal: *Can I come up?* He was a man of few words. Surya was asleep so she decided to go downstairs. Perhaps Himal could offer her comforting distraction.

He saw her among the faces of a group of girls leaving the residence. She smiled on seeing him, but looked troubled.

'Why the long face, beautiful?' Himal lightly kissed her lips and she hugged his chest.

'Can't I stay in your arms forever and never deal with the real world?'

'Honey, this is real and it's all yours. But first tell me what you are running away from.' He put his arm around her waist to lead her back inside.

'No, Himal, we can't go upstairs. Surya is sleeping. She's had a rough day.' Anjani wasn't sure how to tell him what might be happening.

'OK ... Is she doing alright?'

'Not really. We just realised something. Himal ... Surya might be pregnant. From the rape.' There, she'd said it. 'And I don't know how I'm going to deal with that, let alone be there for her.'

Himal looked into her anxious face. She had been through so much already this year. He wished he could take away her troubles, but she loved her twin sister a great deal. Her devotion to Surya was inspirational.

'Slow down, OK. Do you know for sure? Has she taken a test?'

'Well, no, but she hasn't had a … umm … you-know-what in three months!' She looked away. She remembered the first time she and Surya had got their periods. They were twelve years old and their father had just asked if they were OK. That was the first and last time he'd ever said anything about their monthly cycle. Here stood the first man Anjani had discussed menstruation with since then.

'So she hasn't done a test. Well you don't know anything for sure until she takes a test. We can go and buy one of those home tests at the pharmacy now if you want.'

Grateful for his practicality, Anjani accompanied him to the pharmacy. He was right. There was no point in getting all worked up about something that might not be true. The rape and related stress could have easily messed up Surya's monthly cycle. She had to find a way to convince her to take the test in the morning.

–

Anjani sat next to Suraya, pregnancy test in her hand. The sooner they had a result, the sooner they could deal with the consequences. Best-case scenario: Surya was not pregnant and she could go on picking up the pieces of her life as a survivor. Worst case scenario: Surya was pregnant and they had to work through her options together with her counsellor.

'Give it to me.' Surya sat up, her hand outstretched. 'Let's get this over with.'

This was easier than Anjani thought it would be. She was amazed at how much her sister had grown up and become a stronger woman this year.

After reading the instruction leaflet, Surya went to the bathroom and shut the door. Anjani couldn't help but pace. In less than five minutes, their lives could change forever. It was the longest five minutes she'd ever had to wait.

Ten minutes passed. Was Surya still on the toilet? Should she knock on the door? Five more minutes passed. There was no sound from the bathroom. Anjani had to know what was going on.

'Surya, are you all right in there?' She knocked on the door. There was no answer. Panic rose in her chest. 'Surya, is it OK if I come in?' Still no answer.

Anjani opened the door. Surya was sitting on the cold floor, hugging her knees again. Then Anjani saw the test. Two blue lines marked the test window. Surya's pregnancy was confirmed.

Anjani didn't know what to say. The world seemed to cave in on them. Surya was in her arms again. How unfair life could be. Surely they weren't supposed to deal with such tragedies so young? Then again, many other teenagers were born into violence and abuse and grew up expecting the worst out of life. This pregnancy was not something Surya had asked for – especially not from the person who had violated her. What was going through her sister's head? A growing tummy would be a constant reminder of the rape. Could Surya handle that? They had to seek help.

'Surya, I know things can't get any worse right now, but you have some major decisions to make. The sooner we talk to Dr Brown and Sister Johannes, the sooner you can make decisions that will work for you. I know this is an impossible situation, but I'm right here with you. Don't you ever forget that, OK?' Anjani was out of her depth though. Perhaps it was time she sought counselling herself. She knew she was going to need it.

–

The little girl had pink silk ribbons in her hair. She was playing in a garden. The grass was not an ordinary green – it glowed. She was a beautiful child with long brown hair that curled at the ends. She was talking to an imaginary friend and pouring tea into a cup. She offered her friend some biscuits.

'Strawberry-jam biscuits are my favourite!' she was saying. 'But these custard ones are just as nice.'

Her face glowed and Surya's eyes caught the golden glint from sparkly gems on her shoes. She noticed Surya and came running towards her, biscuits in hand.

'I'm so glad you could make it. Come into my garden. You will be happy here. Would you like some tea?' She spoke surprisingly well for a child who couldn't be more than four.

Surya sat down in quiet amazement. She felt an angelic presence around this child. 'Who are you, little one?' she asked, finally finding her words.

'What a silly question!' the girl laughed. 'Well, I have a real question for you, my dear.'

How amusing, thought Surya. She is calling me her 'dear'.

'Would you like me to come to you? Think carefully before you answer. Things will be different with me around.' The angel closed her

grey eyes and smiled into the sun. Her glow grew brighter as if she had summoned energy from the sun.

'Of course I want you with me!' Surya replied without hesitation. 'You're an angel.' It was hard to believe the closeness she felt to this radiant child.

'Then it's done. I will come with you. You have made up your mind.' The angel closed her eyes and smiled into the sun again.

It was so bright that Surya couldn't see anything but she didn't want to look away. She wanted to spend more time with the angel. But it was too bright. She had to close her eyes.

ESOTERIC ENLIGHTENMENT

The room was a dull grey. Surya shifted in her bed. What a strangely beautiful dream. She didn't understand it but she wanted to feel the warmth of that little angel again. It was only five in the morning. She would tell Anjani when she woke. Perhaps her twin could make sense of it all. Then the image of two blue lines on the pregnancy test came back to her. All the bright thoughts of her dream evaporated as she realised what life had thrown into her lap. Perhaps the dream was a form of escape from reality. Surya closed her eyes again, willing the happy child to come back into her thoughts.

It was past eight when Surya stirred again out of restless sleep. Anjani was not in her bed. She was probably at her first lecture of the day. It occurred to Surya that everything that had happened to her had taken its toll on Anjani too yet, despite all the drama, Anjani managed to go to her early morning lectures and keep up with her studies. She even had a love interest. Surya was so proud of her sister and even a little jealous. If the tables were turned, she doubted she would have been as supportive. Anjani had always been the stronger one.

In any case Surya wouldn't wish her situation on anyone. Not even her worst enemy. The bright little girl jumped back into her thoughts. Again, Surya wondered who she was and what the dream meant. She decided to wait for Anjani to come back to res so she could tell her all about it. In the meantime, she tried to focus on her lecture notes but everything she read seemed to disappear before she could understand it. She was staring out the window when Anjani walked into their room at lunchtime.

'Hey, you're here. How are you feeling?' Anjani was surprised to see Surya sitting at her desk.

'Finally, you're back! I had a weird dream last night and I need you to make sense of it all.' Surya moved to her bed and beckoned her sister to sit next to her.

'OK, what did you dream?' It was unlike Surya to remember her dreams, but Anjani was eager to hear about it.

Surya described the angel child who invited her for tea. She also mentioned the question the child had asked her – and the answer she had given. Anjani listened in silence and thought carefully about it when Surya was done.

'Well, do you think you know what it meant? You know about this kind of stuff. What do you think?' Surya was secretly hoping for a sign to show her the way forward. What if the dream was her sign?

'That was quite a profound dream. But I am afraid to tell you what I think it means because I don't think you will like it … I know you are hurting and I don't want to put any ideas in your head.' Anjani was almost certain that this was a sign from a higher being, but Surya was in no state to handle such information.

'No Jenny, you have to tell me what you think. You can't leave me hanging. You've spent years reading about decoding dreams and stuff. I think this one was an important dream, but I don't know for sure. Why else would I have remembered it? If you don't help me, then I have to go and find someone else to help me understand.' Surya was desperate enough to visit a mystic, even though she doubted their abilities.

'Oh no, no, no. You don't know who would be conning you and telling you all sorts of rubbish. OK, I'll tell you what I think from what I've read. But promise me you will keep an open mind. And that you will think carefully about the decisions you have to make with your pregnancy. We are going to see Dr Brown later today. I don't want you to discard any advice he gives you because of this dream. You must remember that you are in control of your life.'

'OK, OK, whatever. Now tell me.'

'OK, here's what I think. You had a visitation from the soul residing within you. I know that you didn't choose what happened to you this year; you know what I mean. But that soul chose you, and may have made her choice to stay with you. Our Hindu scriptures say that a soul hovers above her mother for the first few weeks of the pregnancy until she makes her choice to stay. I don't know how you feel about this baby, given the circumstances, but I think this soul came to you in a dream to ask whether or not you would have her as part of your life. And you said yes. You felt immense love for her, even though you haven't met her yet. That is the profound thing here.'

'Now I could be completely wrong and the dream could just be an escape from all your sadness and trauma. It could be a longing that you have to return to your young self. That is what Western dream dictionaries might say. But I believe you had a visitation from your unborn child. And you chose to keep her in your life. But Surya, like I said before, you'll be given options today at counselling. You will have to decide whether you want to keep this pregnancy or terminate it. That is your decision and I'll support you either way.' Anjani knew in her heart that Surya didn't want this child and nobody could blame her for wanting to end the pregnancy. But she believed that the child had reached out and was meant to be born

'I am so confused, Anjani!' She had never followed Hindu scriptures as closely as her sister. As a little girl, Anjani read everything in sight and asked a million questions until she understood each line of the Bhagavad Gita. Even Nanima got tired of answering her questions. But the words were too much for Surya and the meanings too abstract.

–

Surya's ultrasound established that she was twelve weeks pregnant. They heard the heartbeat racing inside her womb and they watched as the little body swam inside her amniotic fluid. It was eight centimetres long and its body resembled a complete yet miniature human being. Surya didn't know what to feel. The little life form inside her was innocent, but it came to her through such sickening conditions. How was she supposed to accept and love this being?

The twins sat in front of Dr Brown in his office. Sister Johannes had given him a full report of the ultrasound.

'Surya, how are you feeling today?' He sounded gentle.

Surya cut straight to the point. 'Doctor what are my options?'

'Well, it's important for you to know all the facts before you come to any decision. I understand you want to discuss the possibility of termination. Let me talk you through the process.'

As Dr Brown went on to discuss her options, Surya zoned out. The ultrasound had left her numb. Her anxiety from the rape threatened to resurface at any moment.

'I know this is a lot to consider.' Dr Brown was still talking. Surya tried to tune him back in. 'As I said, if you are considering terminating this pregnancy, you don't have too much time – a week at most – before your health could be compromised. My assistant will recommend a registered centre for you to have the procedure if you so wish.'

Surya's brain was tired. All she had done for the last few months was think and work through her emotions. They exhausted her. Her head was filled with the image of her moving baby. It was innocent in all of this. What right did she have to end its life? Then again, what right did its father have to ruin her life? Her anger was building up again. How dare this happen to her?

When they left, she banged her fists on the wall of the counselling building. Anjani grabbed her hands.

'It's OK. Let it out. Let it all out.'

She buried her face in Anjani's chest and let out a muffled scream. They stood there for a while. Surya cried again, until she had no more tears.

Two days went by. For Surya, time became a blur once more. She kept remembering her ultrasound and the little human being growing inside her. She remembered her dream of the glowing child who had asked for permission to come to her. She was an angel; how could Surya consider killing her? But what if that was nothing more than a dream? Surya didn't want this child. She hadn't asked to be raped. She hadn't asked to be pregnant. She wanted to put this year behind her. She even considered what her parents had said about going back home and studying there. It seemed like a welcome offer now.

'I've made my decision,' she announced. Anjani lifted her head from her notes.

'I am going to have the procedure and end this. I've made up my mind. I'll call the abortion centre tomorrow and schedule for next week.'

'Are you sure?'

'Oh, don't ask me if I'm sure. I'm not sure whether I am coming or going!' That was the truth. Surya didn't know if it was the right decision. It just seemed like the most logical one.

Anjani didn't say another word. She knew she had to respect her sister's decision despite what she believed. She felt the urge to visit a shrine and pray. She needed to deal with her own emotions.

'I'm going out for a walk. I'll see you at supper.' She was out the door before Surya could ask where she was going. Anjani had to admit that she had more questions than answers about the events that had taken over their lives. Everything she held dear about her origins and her Hindu beliefs seemed to come under scrutiny as a result of what Surya had gone through.

Why did she have to be raped? Was it a terrible random event or the result of her past karma? How could any God allow such a thing as rape to be conceived in the human mind and body? How could a child be born of such an atrocity? Anjani recalled how many a priest had spoken of the present age of Kali Yuga, a period characterised by an increase in appalling behaviours and a general decrease in virtue and peaceful coexistence. In the Bhagavad Gita, even Lord Krishna referred to the 5000 years of Kali Yuga, which would cause vast suffering for all life on Earth. That certainly described the times in which they lived.

WHOSE LIFE IS IT ANYWAY?

The pink and white stripes of her sneakers moved slowly across the clean, white tiles of the abortion centre. Despite Anjani's insistence on being present, Surya had to go through the termination on her own. The nurse smiled as she stepped into a waiting room. Why would anyone working in such a morbid place have any reason to be happy? The nurse was mouthing words. Surya heard nothing, but her lips were moving in response. Something about pain management. Then the nurse was walking away. The procedure had to take place to put an end to this chapter of a horrible year. An unwanted pregnancy would not allow Surya to move forward.

They were in a different room now. The walls were a sickly hospital blue that almost turns grey if you stare at it for too long. The smiley nurse was back and asked Surya to change into a hospital gown. It was time for one more ultrasound to make sure that an abortion could take place. The anaesthetist wheeled in his drip. He was almost a non-person: covered from head to toe in blue overalls with a white cap on his head, all that remained visible were his grey eyes. To him Surya was just another patient who needed to be monitored and administered the exact amount of anaesthetic. Long sterile needles lay on a stainless steel table on bleached towels. Surya was on the cold hospital bed for a long time as everyone set up around her. Surreal despair kicked in. Waiting sucked. It seemed like this entire year couldn't have happened. Did it all really happen? The rape? The fighting with Mummy? This pregnancy? Intense pain from her clenched jaw released the tears.

The stocky Dr March acknowledged her with a grunt. He wasn't as friendly as the nurse or Sister Johannes. The physical invasion began when the icy, clear lubricant touched her skin. Dr March's total lack of emotion didn't ease the pressure building inside Surya. He nodded to the anaesthetist and walked over to his needles. Wasn't anyone going to say anything to her or at least explain the procedure? She looked up into the screen. There was the little life, swimming freely inside her womb. It wasn't created out of love but it was innocent. It hadn't harmed her. It was looking to her for nourishment and love. And she was about to kill it. How could she live with that? And what about her dream – the angel that had invited herself into Surya's life? That did it.

Surya jumped off the doctor's table. The scanning apparatus flew out of his hand and hit the monitor. He caught it on its rebound towards him and peered up at her.

'I can't do this. I can't do it. I'm sorry to waste your time, Doctor.'

Surya didn't wait for his response. She knew this was a mistake. It was so clear to her now. The surgeon and anaesthetist just looked resigned. They had probably seen many women changing their minds at the last minute.

She pulled on her track pants and sweat top, anxious to get out of there.

Despite all Surya's protestations, Anjani was still waiting outside the abortion centre, but Surya was so glad to see her she didn't mind.

'Jenny, I couldn't do it. I don't care what happens to me, but I can't abort this baby. I'm sorry.'

Anjani hugged her sister. Her eyes were flooded with tears, but she was smiling.

'Don't be sorry. Please don't be sorry. This is your child. I know you'll protect it. We'll protect her together!' Anjani's prayers had been answered. She wiped away her tears.

'Her, hey? How come you're so sure it's a her?' Surya was so relieved to have her twin by her side.

'Your dream, silly. Remember? She has already come to you.' Anjani was beaming. She was so sure of the signs of Surya's dreams. 'Remember what Nanima used to tell us – that each of us has a special purpose on this earth?'

'Ya, and she said that mine was to create mischief!'

'Well, maybe she was right. Not about you creating mischief, but about each of us having a purpose. Maybe this child you are carrying has a special purpose. You mustn't forget that. Only time will tell.'

Surya ignored her sister's comments about what this baby might be. She didn't even know what the baby would look like, but she felt empowered for reasons she couldn't explain.

'You know what? I think you chose the wrong profession. You should have become a soothsayer. It suits you!' She smiled as Anjani play-slapped her shoulder.

'It's good to see you smile again, you know.' Anjani hugged her as they walked down to their dorm room, both acutely aware of the struggles ahead, but willing to deal with them.

–

'How is Surya? And you?' said Nirmala. The girls had asked her to phone them this evening.

'We are OK. Trying to get back into my books properly. And Surya is still catching up with her lectures.' Anjani was making small talk to avoid the bomb that was about to explode.

'Your'll eating properly? Must I freeze and send some more roti and curry?' Nirmala knew this wasn't the reason her daughters asked her to phone them. 'So, what happened now?'

'Well, Surya is doing better, but we found out something the other day. I think she wants to speak to you herself. Hold on.' Anjani thought it was best that Surya spoke to their mother. It was her way of taking back control in her life. Anjani was proud of her.

'Hello, Ma. H-how are you?' Surya felt nervous. Their conversations had never been the same since the rape. They were always avoiding the giant elephant in the room.

'I'm fine. Now, you want to tell me what's going on? Has something happened to you again?' Nirmala wanted the truth out. She wished she could see her daughters' faces.

'Well, yes, something has happened. We didn't expect this.' Surya stopped short. She took in a deep breath. 'I found out the other day. I'm pregnant. From the rape.' It was the first time she'd told anyone that she was pregnant.

Nirmala sat down on her bed. This couldn't be happening to her. Not again.

'What do you mean? How do you know?' Perhaps it was all a mistake.

'Well, we realised I had missed my period for three months.

So Jenny got me a home test. It was positive. And we had a scan at the Health Centre. The baby is over twelve weeks now. Mummy, I am as shocked as you are. I didn't expect this at all.' Surya was reaching out to her mother. She wanted her support more than anything else.

'You didn't expect this? How could you not expect this? You slept with a man! I can't listen to this any more!' She handed the phone to Ashok.

'Hello, Jenny. What's wrong?' Ashok knew something was seriously amiss from the look on his wife's face.

'No Dad, it's me, Surya. And I don't know why I expected any sympathy from Mummy. She thinks I slept with a man.' Surya handed the phone to Anjani and left the room.

'Hello, Daddy? What did she say?' Anjani couldn't believe her mother had let Surya down again.

'Jenny, what's going on? What did Surya say to Mummy?'

'Dad, Surya is pregnant. We found out a few days ago and we did all the tests. She is just over twelve weeks. It was from the rape.' Anjani didn't know why she had to justify Surya's pregnancy. 'I thought Mummy would've been more understanding. What did she say to Surya? She's so upset that she's walked out the room.'

'I don't know. I came in here and she handed me the phone. This is a big shock for us.' But Ashok wasn't surprised. He had thought of this possibility before and hoped it wouldn't come true.

'Well, we need to see you soon. We must decide as a family what to do about raising this child.' Anjani was trying to hold back the emotion in her voice. 'Oh, and Dad? Surya almost had an abortion. But she couldn't go through with it. And I agree with her. This child is innocent in all of this.'

'Even if it brings shame on this family? That is what your mother is afraid of – dealing with the questions and comments from the family and the neighbours.' He knew his wife's anxieties all too well.

'Daddy, you don't honestly expect me to care about that now? I have to be here for Surya and try to finish my studies. And to tell you the truth, I don't know how I am going to manage. What about Surya? She is going to be so fragile when her stomach starts showing. I don't know what she is going to do about her courses this year.' Anjani was only just realising the extent to which their lives were going to change over the coming months.

'Calm down. I'll book a flight. I'll let you know when I am coming. Look after yourself, OK?' Ashok had to get to his daughters. He put the phone down and sat next to his wife. 'What did you say to her? She left the dorm room.' He thought Nirmala knew better. Surya was dealing with so much.

'What am I going to do? It's one big headache after the next with this girl. She's a curse on this family, you know that?' Nirmala thought how much better it would have been if she didn't have daughters. Sons didn't bring so much shame.

'How can you keep saying that? That means you still think she asked to be raped, huh?' He was starting to understand Anjani's point of view. Surya wanted her family's support, but all she got was her mother's distrust. 'Well, I'm going to see them. Must I book for you too?'

'Hm, how can you ask me like that? Go! Go on your own and support your shameless daughters. It's because of you they have no cares in this world even if they do so much wrong!' A deep ache rose in her belly again. Her husband loved rescuing his darlings and never stood by her in disciplining the girls, especially Surya.

'Fine. I'll go.' There was no doubt that Surya had given Nirmala most of her grey hairs over the years, but he wondered how a mother could so easily believe the worst about her own child.

This trip had to be carefully timed. He had to let Nirmala cool down a little or risk her blood pressure rising beyond control. If she drove around town with a high blood pressure, she would be a danger to herself.

–

Surya's phone vibrated. It was an SMS: *Please come back to the room. We can go out for a pizza together and talk. Love, A.*

Anjani to the rescue. She started making her way back to the dorm. It was getting cold outside and her cheeks were crusty with dried tears. As she wiped her face, her mother's words played in her head over and over again: *You slept with a man!*

She had said it with so much revulsion. Surya was convinced her mother hated her and wished she had never been born. She wondered if this was the way she was going to feel about her own child. Her hand instinctively fell on her tummy. She made up her mind to believe in this child no matter what the family thought. She would break the cycle of shame. She would raise her child differently.

Yet she had to admit that all she wanted right now was the comfort of her family. Anjani was her angel, always by her side, but she wanted her parents' love and Nanima's special care. Perhaps she should go home and speak to them in person. She would make them understand.

'Jenny, I think I need to go home,' said Surya when she walked into their room.

'Home? But Dad's already coming here. He's probably booking a flight right now.'

'I need to see Mummy ... and Nanima.'

'Are you sure about that? Do you want to deal with Mummy's verbal abuse?'

'I have to make them understand my reasons for keeping this child. Mummy needs to hear – from my mouth – what happened to me and I need to do this in person. Maybe then she will realise that I didn't choose to be raped or to be pregnant.' Surya was scared, but this felt right. 'I'm not sure if it'll work, but I have to try. She is, after all, our mother.'

Surya made a good point. Mummy had always come around no matter how bad things got with Surya. This was no doubt the most traumatic of events and it would take time for everybody to heal, but the family needed to stick together.

THE GIANT ELEPHANT IN THE ROOM

Surya didn't have to work hard at convincing Ashok to book her flight back to Durban in two weeks' time. He longed to see her and by then Surya would be out of the development phase of her baby's life and safe to travel by air. She also approached the dean to defer her exams until the following year. He was well aware of the events she'd endured and agreed to allow her to write the supplementary exams next January. His decision helped ease some of Surya's tension.

Durban was green. Always on time, the November rains had swallowed up the brown of winter. The palm trees and sugar-cane fields up the sides of the hilly terrain welcomed a washing away of winter dust and dryness. As Amos, the family's trusty driver, sped down the highway, Surya touched the bump on her belly. This was going to be a strange visit to her childhood home. Eight months ago, she'd left it as a carefree young girl. Now she returned as a heavy-hearted, swollen-bellied woman.

There was nobody in sight as they pulled up to the main entrance. The creamy marble columns she and Anjani used to dance around as children gleamed in the sunlight. Things were so much simpler back then.

'Hello, anybody home?' Maybe she sounded too cheery. 'Mummy? Nanima?'

She heard familiar footsteps. They were getting faster.

'Surya? What are you doing here?' Nirmala gasped when she saw her daughter standing in the doorway. 'Did anyone see you? Quickly, get inside!' She noticed the bump in her daughter's stomach. She wondered why Surya would wear a form-fitting T-shirt when she was already showing.

'Hello to you too, Ma!' Was it always going to be like this between them?

'Listen Surya, I don't know why your father didn't tell me you were coming. I would have told him that you should've stayed that side, far away from here!' Nirmala was wringing a dishtowel to death.

'Ma, I wanted to see you in person. We have to talk about this as a family. I know you are upset, but you need to hear everything from me, so you can understand.'

'Oh, I know you very well. You may have changed by going to university and getting pregnant, but you are still that same old scheming child of mine!' Nirmala wasn't going to listen to Surya this time. 'Can you see? Look at my face! Look at my hair! You have put me in this state since primary school. You've left the house and you are still doing it. And now you want to talk? Hm!'

Her mother had aged considerably since Surya had last seen her. Her heart sank from disappointment in herself. The corners of her mother's mouth and eyes had fine lines that grew deeper as she spoke, and her hair was coarser with sprouts of grey creeping out. She was hoping that a heart-to-heart would help ease her mother's stress levels.

'Ma, let's sit down. I am not playing mind games with you. I want to tell you everything as I remember it so you will know I didn't do anything to bring this onto our family. It was my bad luck that I was chosen as his ... as my rapist's victim.' It was still hard for Surya to talk about the rape, but she was willing to bare her heart to her mother.

She sat down but Nirmala was hesitant to sit next to her daughter. Their awkwardness was broken by slower footsteps. Surya stared into the face of her grandmother. She smiled.

'Nanima, I'm home!' Surya got up to hug her.

Nanima stepped away from Surya's outstretched arms.

'Arre Raam, what have you come here for? Look what you have done to this family. You broke it up!' Nanima struggled to catch her breath. Nirmala helped her to sit down.

Surya could not believe her only living grandparent could be so cold and unloving. She tried to hide her shock and took in a deep breath before sitting back down.

'I understand. You don't want anyone to know about what happened to me. But I want you to know that I didn't ask for this. I didn't ask for that rapist to pick me. But he did and now I am carrying his child. There's nothing you or I can do about it. We have to ... we have to work through this as a family. Can we at least agree on that?'

'So you go and expose your body to the world. You dress and dance like a slut in front of all these dirty men. God knows what you were drinking or smoking. You've got that rubbish friend Ashraf – Ash, you call him – who smokes dagga and you want us to work through your unwanted pregnancy as a family? What do you think – we were born yesterday? Wake up my girl, you got yourself into this mess, you can deal with it on your own!'

Nirmala was appalled by her audacity in assuming that the family would accept her mess and help her out.

'So what are you saying? That all of this is my fault? Didn't you speak to Dr Brown? I am not the first girl to get raped like this. It has happened on campuses all over the country, even here in Durban. It wasn't my behaviour that brought this on. He stole all of my things too. You know that!'

'Dr Brown, my foot! He doesn't know your history. But we know you and I'm sure you're not one of a kind. There are plenty of bitchy girls like you everywhere. We have seen them on TV and what happens to them! All your life I tried to warn you. I tried to talk to you how many times! And every time you went running to your daddy and manipulated him against me. Well, not any more. He thinks that by you coming here we are going to forgive you and accept the disgrace you bring into this house. Well both of you can forget it.' Nirmala stood up. She had nothing more to say.

'Where are you going? I want you to hear everything. I know I haven't been the easiest daughter in the world. I know I was naughty. But I promise you I never asked to be raped. Never. I was always careful. I still don't know what happened that night because whoever did this drugged me. They tested my blood and proved it. That is why I can't remember anything except waking up in that place.' Surya's eyes were wet with tears.

'Enough, Surya! Enough. I don't want to hear any more. Do you know how sick I have been since you brought this on us? Do you know how sick Nanima has been? She is getting old now. We can't deal with your nonsense any more. You must go back to varsity. You can't stay here. I don't want the whole neighbourhood to see your big stomach!'

'So that's it! You are going to send me back because you are so worried about what the family and the neighbours are going to say? You don't care that I want you to be a part of my life, and this baby's life?'

'I don't want any part of that child's life! How can you even ask me that? Sis! You messed up all of our lives and you want us to pretend like everything is OK. I don't know what I did to deserve this. I never ill-treated you. Your father and I and Nanima gave you everything of the best. And this is how you repay us? By shaming us in front of the whole world!' Nirmala had to sit down. She was dizzy. White spots were appearing in her vision. Her blood pressure was on the rise.

Nanima went to her. 'Look what you've done now!' she yelled at Surya. 'You caused your Mummy enough trouble. Get out! Ja!' Nanima spoke Hindi to the girls only when she was very angry. When she said, 'Ja', there was no arguing with her.

Surya watched her grandmother fuss over her mother. She'd never meant to cause them pain or humiliation. Why couldn't they see that this wasn't her intention? Nanima turned and glared at her.

'What you still sitting here for? I said get out! Your mother doesn't want you in this house. You rubbish girl. Go!' Nanima took her arm, her bony fingers jabbing into Surya's skin. She tightened her grip and got Surya to her feet. 'And don't come back here. You are not from this family any more, you hear me? Ja!' Nanima pulled Surya out the front door and let go of her arm as her feet got to the marble floor. She reached for the door.

'No, Nanima, please listen to me. Why won't you believe me?' Surya could hardly speak.

'Go from here. And take your shame with you. Your mother

has had enough of you. We don't want any baby from you. You want to keep your baby? Then you have to go!' Nanima shut the door. Surya heard her shouting for Amos.

She gave up her protest and went back to the car. Amos took her to the airport. He was quiet the whole way but was kind enough to offer Surya a tissue for her tears. She thought about phoning her father, but what was the use? Her maternal family had discarded her.

–

Meanwhile, a nosy face poked out of her kitchen window to see the commotion unfold at the mansion next door.

'You know, not too long ago, I saw Nirmala and Ashok running out the house. Promise, you remember that?' Mrs Naidoo was about to begin an inquisition.

Promise was ironing in the kitchen and had nowhere to escape to. 'Yes madam.' She didn't like it when Mrs Naidoo wanted to talk about Amos' bosses. Amos was a good man and she liked him. He liked her too. They looked forward to their evening meetings in his outhouse room.

'Now, didn't I see Surya came way home? What she's doing here? It's not the end of term yet. Ayo, maybe she got expelled. So many times that happened at school, but her father bought the principal and all. Now who's going to save her, so far she is.'

'Hayibo, madam. I don't know.' Promise played ignorant. She didn't like to gossip.

'You don't know. Where you don't know? I know you visit Amos at night. He told you something. Why you lying to me? You know I pay you very nicely and you get nice food here.

What, that's not enough for you to tell me one little thing, eh?' Making Promise feel guilty always worked.

'Ow, madam. Angaazi. I didn't see Amos yesterday.' Mrs Naidoo's mouth curled up crookedly at the right corner. She always got nasty when she had that look. 'Ya, but he went to the airport, Madam.'

'Aha, so it must have been Surya I saw. I wonder why she came home now. You don't know?'

'No, madam.' Promise tried hard to concentrate on the fold of Mr Naidoo's shirt to avoid any more of Mrs Naidoo's upturned lip.

THE INN – INDIAN NEWS NETWORK:
A BROADCAST OF A DIFFERENT KIND

Ashok was disappointed in his wife and her mother. Surya had made the effort to reach out to them. She needed their support. Whether the pregnancy was unwanted or not, it was a new and overwhelming time in Surya's young life. Ashok took comfort in the fact that Anjani was close to her sister, but the whole experience would take its toll on her too. He continued to send extra money to his daughters, but he had to think of a way to keep them protected, especially when the baby arrived.

Mrs Naidoo couldn't have asked for a juicier situation. She was in the right place at the right time to find out the truth about Surya that day. Promise never checked the washing once she'd hung it up. Mrs Naidoo had to go and turn the washing so that the sun would dry everything, and the Naidoos' washing line hung conveniently close to the fence that overlooked the Harsinghs' mansion. And Mrs Naidoo caught a glimpse of *her*.

Surya was crying and holding her stomach. Her grandmother was shouting at her. Mrs Naidoo's ears pricked up. What was she saying?

'Go from here. And take your shame with you. Your mother

has had enough of you. We don't want any baby from you. You want to keep your baby? Then you have to go!'

Did she hear right? A baby? Surya was pregnant? That must be why she was holding her stomach. But her stomach wasn't showing. She must have just found out and come to tell her mother. What a thing! And now they had kicked her out of the house.

Mrs Naidoo ran into her room. She was going to choose her best sari for the prayers at the temple tomorrow. She couldn't wait to tell her friends what she'd seen and heard next door.

The next evening, Mrs Naidoo arrived early at the temple. It was a weekday so there wouldn't be too many people, but she'd telephoned Mrs Pather and Mrs Chand to make sure they would come. She had big news for them.

As people filled the temple hall, the priest began reciting his mantras. A large wall hanging of Lord Ganesha hung from the ceiling to the floor of the stage. The smell of beans curry and puri cooked on open fires outside filled their senses, along with the agarbathi that wafted around the hall. Mrs Naidoo sat right at the back so she could easily spot Mrs Pather and Mrs Chand. When she finally saw them, she beckoned them to sit next to her.

'So what's all this big news you got?' said Mrs Pather.

'Yah, why you didn' say over the phone?' added Mrs Chand.

Mrs Naidoo took a deep breath. 'Listen to this. You know my neighbour, Mrs Harsingh? She thinks she's so high and mighty in her mansion. And your'll know her two daughters? Surya and Anjani.' The two ladies nodded. 'Surya the very naughty one. Yah, well yesterday I was hanging the washing—'

'How come you hanging the washing? What happened to Promise?' Mrs Chand chipped in.

'Wait let her finish telling the story first,' said Mrs Pather.

Her husband was good friends with the twins' father. She wanted to know what had happened to them.

'Yah, you know that Promise. She's one dilly thing. And lazy. She don' check the washing. She just leaves it and then it's half dry so she don' have ironing to do and can go early. So, I was turning the washing and then I saw Surya come out of the mansion. Her granny was so angry with her. I wondered what she did now and why she was home in the middle of term. Then I heard the granny.'

Mrs Naidoo's storytelling abilities had her friends' full attention. 'What the granny said? She very fussy that old aunty.' Mrs Chand recalled an earlier incident when she was doing the measles prayer for her son and had to ask for flour and sugar from different homes. The old granny looked her up and down like she was dirty or something. And so rich they are, but the granny only gave one small packet of each thing. Such a miser she was.

'The granny said she don' want any baby from Surya. And that Surya must take her shame and go way from their house. Imagine: she kicked her own granddaughter out the house. What your'll think about that?' Mrs Naidoo finished her story with a sense of triumph and reached into her bag on the floor for a tissue. 'The grand mansion with the perfect family is not so perfect. And to think I wanted my Savathri to join those girls. Lucky she didn' want. Otherwise I would have also had one headache at home with a big stomach.'

Her friends didn't say anything in response to her big news.

'So what your'll think about that?' she repeated.

She looked up into their awkward faces. Standing next to them was Nirmala Harsingh.

'How dare you spread gossip about my family?'

Mrs Naidoo didn't have an answer.

'You know, what happens in my yard is my family's business. You don' know what you talking about. So stop telling other people lies.'

But it was the truth and now the whole community would hear about it. Nirmala's cheeks were burning as she walked away, defeated. There was no point trying to pray for inner peace from Ganeshji now. The whole world would hear via the three biggest gossipmongers in the neighbourhood how her daughter went to university and fell pregnant in her first year. And there was nothing she could do to stop the gossip from spreading.

'Oh, Ganapati help me,' she whispered under her breath. Life was about to turn upside down.

AN UNEXPECTED ARRIVAL

Surya stared into the mirror. Not too long ago, she would have admired her toned physique. The pregnancy had left her so worn out she could not manage more than a little stretching in terms of exercise. Her bump had grown into a mountain. A mountain of uncertainty. Any day now, her water would break and she would have to push out an unknown part of her. This morning, the cramps were stronger and deeper inside her. She was particularly miserable these days with the extra weight of her baby. She found herself thinking more and more about what it would be like to end her life.

Her headaches had returned with a vengeance. Her family didn't want her. She didn't want to raise a child. All she had was Anjani. Perfect Anjani. With her flawless skin and perfect little body. *Why did this have to happen to me? Why couldn't it have happened to Anjani?* Then everyone would stop thinking she was perfect. Surya was burning holes into a picture of Anjani and herself when her twin walked in.

'Hello beautiful. How are you feeling today?' Anjani thought Surya had an unmistakeable maternal glow, despite her depression.

'Quit calling me beautiful. Look at you! With your skinny

legs and short skirt. I want that back. And since when do you dress like that anyways? Do you know what your mother would say if she saw you looking like that?'

'She's your mother also. And yes, I know what she would say. Who you parading for? You think you one film star now?' Anjani gave a hearty laugh.

Surya did not find her sister's imitation of their mother amusing. 'Well, maybe she'll disown you too! Then you won't think it's so funny.'

'Nobody's disowned you, Surya! Daddy still cares for us and he still phones us. And I am here with you!' Anjani was getting tired of Surya's negativity, but she couldn't blame her.

'Yeah, why are you still here? Surely you want to go back to Mummy dearest and show her what a good daughter you are! You're still studying; hell, you even managed a first-class pass last year! Oh, but don't tell her about Himal. She'll probably kill you for looking at a man. And then she'll ask you when your baby is due! Or maybe not. In their eyes, you could never do anything wrong.'

'Hey, watch it, missy. Our mother doesn't speak to me either, you know. Because I support you and she's too pig-headed to do the same. They think I have a big mouth and being here with you is wrong.'

'Oh shame, you poor thing. Mummy doesn't talk to you. What are you going to do? Why don't you run off to her and beg her forgiveness? She'll take you back into her arms in an instant. And she'll be happy that you left me all alone. Because I am the devil incarnate. Arrgh!' Surya felt a sharp pain at the base of her belly. Then a warm liquid flowed down her leg. The floor was wet in front of her feet but she had to sit down.

'Surya, Surya! Are you OK?'

'Get away from me! I'm tired of you mothering me. I'm fine.'
But this pain was more than Braxton-Hicks contractions. It was
deeper.

'Oh, my God! You're not fine. Your water just broke. We have
to get you to the clinic.' Anjani was on the phone before Surya
could protest.

–

The phone vibrated on his desk. It was late afternoon and Ashok
was on his landline to a shirt manufacturer. There were too
many complaints from his retailers about loosely stitched but-
tons. This particular manufacturer was full of excuses. Ashok
never had the heart to cut somebody off, even in business, but
he was glad for the interruption caused by his cell phone. Especially since it was Anjani calling.

'Juggie, I have to go now. Got another call coming through.
Make sure I don't receive any more complaints about your next
batch. Otherwise, we gonna have to talk again. OK? Right, bye.'

He exhaled as he answered Anjani's call. 'Anjani? How you
sweetie?' His girls were his darlings, no matter what anybody said.

'Daddy! You need to come quick. It's Surya. She's in labour
now.'

So the moment had finally arrived. 'Is she doing OK? Are you
at the clinic now?'

'Yes, we're at the clinic. I don't know if she's fine. She's very
angry about all the pain. Is that normal?' Anjani sounded frantic.

*They are just children themselves. I have to go to them. Now
I must face Nirmala and remind her of everything that she wants*

to forget. Ashok exhaled deeply, stretching into the back of his chair. He rubbed his forehead with the palm of his hand and ran his fingers through his thinning hair. How had this family of his gone from unity to such chaos?

'Don't worry, the nurses will tell her what she needs to do. You just be there for her, OK? I'm sorry you have to deal with this on your own. I can only get a flight out tomorrow, now. I have to go home and tell your mother and Nanima.'

'Good luck Daddy. I can't wait to see you again.' Anjani rang off.

Ashok's thoughts raced. That old lady had kicked his own child out of his house. She had no right; it was their house first. But for the sake of peace he kept quiet and kept his distance. There'd been more than one occasion when he'd wanted to give her a piece of his mind, but Nimmie's blood pressure would have sky-rocketed. He had enough problems to deal with and she wouldn't even talk to him much. His own wife, fuelled by that mother of hers, was only giving one-word answers to his questions. Couldn't she see what this was doing to their family?

And Poor Anjani. She'd only come home for one week of her summer holidays. Only one week. She was too afraid to leave Surya at varsity all by herself. And those ladies had made her feel so bad. She'd done nothing wrong. Thee new year was half-finished and she was going to be tested again. He didn't know how his daughters were going to handle having a baby around. He wished they were closer, but Nimmie wanted them to stay away. She was always so worried about the community and saving face. That's what made her blood pressure rise. But he couldn't aggravate the problems by insisting on seeing the twins back home.

Now he had to tell them this news. A baby should be good news, but under the circumstances, how could it be? What happened to his child was a sin, but she shouldn't be the one to be punished for it. It didn't matter now. He was going to his girls no matter what.

–

Nirmala watched as he packed his travel bag. He didn't even know where his own underwear was kept in their room, but he systematically opened all the cupboards until he found it

That was the extent of his dedication to his daughters: he didn't talk to her any more so he wouldn't ask her to help him. She'd given up arguing with him. He was, after all, a good man and a good husband. Everything she'd ever wanted he got for her and he was still so handsome even at his age. On top of all that, he hadn't complained one bit when Ma had come to stay. He could've easily said no, Jignesh must look after her. The looks she'd got from his family. They hadn't wanted Ashok to help Ma but she had nowhere else to go where she could be comfortable and feel like part of the family.

Her stupid brother Jignesh couldn't even get married and was drowning in alcohol half the time. The rest of the time, he pretended to be working at that radio and TV repair shop. He was always on the phone, trying to make back-door deals with other rubbishes. How could she leave Ma with him? She would have had a heart attack or stroke from all Jignesh's goings on. She'd made sure Nirmala got married to a good home. Ashok was the complete opposite of Jignesh: a successful businessman, well respected by everyone in this community. Ma had been so pleased when his family brought the proposal home.

With Baba gone, Ma had managed to throw such a lavish wedding for her. The families couldn't find one bad thing to say about the food or the hall or the bride and groom. Ma had done that for her. Only the best. There was no way she was going to let her suffer with that good-for-nothing son of hers after that. Ashok took her in with open arms. He loved her so much and Ma came at the right time to help her with the girls' birth. She used to massage Nirmala and let her rest while she looked after both girls.

Nirmala had so much to be grateful for but now her husband only lived for their daughters. He could see how her blood pressure rose, but the girls came first.

'When will you be back?' she found herself asking.

He looked up at her hoping this wouldn't turn into an argument. 'I'm not sure. I'll book the return flight after ... well, after I've settled the girls.' Ashok did not want to share too many details of his plans for his daughters.

'Phone me when you get there. And let me know when you coming back.' There was no use trying to change his mind.

LORD GANESHA GOES TO WORK

Nirmala stood in front of her mandir. When Ashok built this house, he knew how important prayer and ritual were to the family, so he gave prominence to the mandir. There were raised platforms tiled in warm cream marble for all the idols that represented the various deities or forms of God. She stood in front of her brass lamp, taking in the sandalwood incense she had lit.

Today was a special day on the Hindu calendar – Ganesh Chaturthi: the birth of Lord Ganesha, the elephant-headed deity who represented wisdom and good fortune. She had offered milk laced with honey, sour milk and sugar candy to their gold and marble idol of Ganesha. He stared back at her through his wise old elephant eyes and garland of velvet red roses. A further sweet offering of laddoos – sweet round ochre balls made from sugar, chickpea flour and almonds, coated in coconut – lay on a brass tray at his feet. Ladoos were fabled to be his favourite sweet treat and the reason for his rather large belly. Lord Ganesha was worshipped for the removal of all obstacles and to ensure his richest blessings to all his devotees.

Nirmala brought the palms of her hands together. Her thoughts of Ashok and Surya disturbed her focus on her prayers, making her more agitated.

O Ganapatibapa, please forgive me for being so upset today. Please forgive me for all that I have done wrong. I don't know what I did to deserve this shame on my family. Please make this mess go away. I am so miserable now. Please make my family right again.

Nanima was sitting cross-legged on the floor. She had been chanting Lord Ganesha's many names from six in the morning. Today she would fast. She would give up salted and unwholesome foods until tomorrow, only taking in fruit, yoghurt and water. Nirmala did not want her mother to hear her prayers for their family.

Yet Nanima's prayers were no different. She chanted Ganesha's 108 names, but her mind was elsewhere. Her granddaughter was in a hospital bed in the Eastern Cape delivering her sin. She too asked Ganeshji why such disgrace had been brought on this family.

–

It was the worst thing Surya had ever had to deal with.

'How are you feeling? It's all over now.' Anjani was cautious.

Surya had screamed through her labour pains. Twelve hours of agony. And in the end she had pushed with fury as if she just wanted the baby out of her. It was a girl. The nurses had taken her away to clean her up and record her birth statistics. Surya had yet to hold her child. Perhaps she would feel differently once that happened.

'I'm exhausted. I need to sleep now. Have they finished with her?' Surya had mixed feelings about her child. She wanted to see her, but she also never wanted to see her again. Sister Johannes was on hand for the morning shift. She came in with a little bundle carefully wrapped in a blanket. She smiled at the sisters.

'Here's your baby girl, all cleaned up and inspected. The paediatrician has checked her. All seems normal and healthy.' She handed the baby to Surya.

Surya did not smile, but she marvelled at her creation. As much as it reminded her of all the pain she had gone through in the last year, the little child was perfect. In fact, she was beautiful. But she could not get too close, she thought. That would be dangerous.

'She's beautiful. Like you, you know,' said Anjani. She couldn't help feeling pride for her sister after everything she had been through. This baby had forced herself into their lives, but it was impossible not to feel her allure.

'Let me show you how to breastfeed her now. She must be hungry,' said Sister Johannes.

'Oh God, no! I don't want to breastfeed. Can you imagine what that would look like?' Surya was beside herself imagining sitting at lectures with her baby pulling at her naked breast.

Sister Johannes was a little startled, but then she remembered the circumstances around this pregnancy and birth. 'I'm sorry. It's all right, I understand. I'll get one of the nurses to bring you a bottle.' She rolled in a crib next to Surya's bed. 'I'll leave you with your baby then.' She hurried off to tend to other patients.

'The nerve of that woman. How can she think that I would want to breastfeed? Really now.' Surya was still imagining drooping breasts and a wailing baby.

'She's just being a nurse. Besides, breast milk is apparently the best milk for a growing baby. That's why they recommend you breastfeed.' Anjani had tried to read up on baby literature in between her course reading. She figured that Surya did not want to think about the baby more than she already did.

'Yeah well, I'm not going to, OK? So drop it.' Surya felt awful. She wanted to sleep. Her baby looked so peaceful sleeping next to her, completely unaware of the panic rising in her mother.

'OK, sorry. Why don't you try to rest for a while? I need to see if Daddy has got here yet. His flight should have landed a while ago.' Anjani needed their father's support.

She looked closer at the little baby lying next to Surya. She was angelic in her sleep, but all of this made Anjani nervous.

As she walked out of the hospital ward, Ashok was walking in. She ran to him. 'I'm so glad you're here,' she sighed as she hugged her father.

'Is everything OK? Surya? The baby?'

'Yes, yes. They are both OK. The baby is … she's beautiful!' Anjani smiled. 'And Surya, well, she's her usual grumpy self, but they're both sleeping now.'

'It's a girl,' he smiled. 'OK, let's leave them to rest. We'll have an early lunch and then we can come back.' Ashok prepared to busy himself. He was nervous for his daughters, but he knew what had to be done.

They made their way to the Mad Hatter's Tea House in town. Rhodes University was one of the main reasons for Grahamstown's existence, but this made the little coffee shops all the more inviting. The locals went the extra mile to offer good service.

'Oh, today's Ganesh Chaturthi. No meat today.' Ashok remembered to tell Anjani before she reminded him.

'OK, I know. Oh, wow, that means Surya's baby was born

on such an auspicious day.' It made the baby girl even more captivating.

'Anjani, I hope you don't think too badly of me. I went ahead and found out the initial of this child's name. I don't think there'll be a proper chatti.' Ashok had phoned the priest as soon as Anjani had told him the time the baby was born.

A chatti or naming ceremony normally took place six days after the birth of a baby. Using Vedic astrology, the pundit would provide the first letters or sounds that the baby's name should begin with according to the time of birth and alignment of the planets. It was usually the child's father's sister who named the new arrival and performed many of the rituals of the naming ceremony. In this case, nobody knew who the father was, let alone if he had a sister. Still, Ashok felt it was right to name the child according to Hindu custom, as his daughters were.

'Daddy, why would I be upset with you? So, tell me: what initial should her name begin with?' Anjani was thrilled at the prospect of finding a name for her new niece.

'"D" or the sound "Dhi", which might be hard for a girl's name.'

'I'll Google Hindu baby names. I'm sure we'll find something.' Anjani thought something related to the holiness of the day would be suitable for Surya's baby.

'You'll what? Googly? What's that?'

'Oh Daddy, you need to catch up on technology,' laughed Anjani. 'What did Surya used to call you? Oh yes, technologically challenged!'

'No, no Googly for me. I'm still happy with my pen and paper, thank you very much.' Ashok was happy to have made his child laugh again.

Back at the hospital, Surya was awake. Her baby was still sleeping next to her. She was exhausted but her mind raced. Now what would happen? Where to from here? How was she supposed to care for this little life? She had to admit there was absolutely nothing wrong with her baby. In fact, she was a gorgeous little girl. Surya had woken up to her meek cry and fed her a bottle of formula milk. She had managed this despite her misgivings about caring for a child. She didn't know the first thing about looking after babies. She watched her baby's chest rise and fall. This little girl was oblivious to the fact that her father was a rapist. She would never know him. And Surya did not consider herself mother material. What was this child's life going to amount to? She regretted her decision not to terminate the pregnancy. But it was too late for that. She had to figure out a way to make this work. She wondered where Anjani and her father had gone. She envied Anjani's freedom again. Then they walked in.

'Hi, new mummy. Did you get some sleep?' Anjani went straight to the baby.

Surya did not like the sound of 'mummy'. She looked up into her father's face.

'Hello,' said Ashok. He was unsure of what to say to his daughter. 'How are you feeling, Surya?' He hugged her.

'I'll feel much better when I can get out of here!' Surya wondered how to introduce the baby to him. Shame overwhelmed her.

'Daddy, meet your … your granddaughter,' said Anjani. 'Isn't she beautiful?'

Surya waited for her father's reaction. She hated Anjani's cheerfulness right now. This was an awkward situation and Anjani wasn't helping with her positive attitude.

'Hello, little one.' Ashok's heart melted. It was like reliving the birth of the twins. They'd been tinier than this little girl, but she had the same effect. She was pure joy. She was baby Surya all over again. How could he feel any different?

Surya heaved a sigh of relief at her father's reaction. That was one less thing to worry about.

'She's going to be a good baby, I can tell,' he said. 'You girls were screaming at me from the start!' He had broken the tension. Now was a good time to tell them. 'Listen, girls, I made arrangements for your'll. Surya, you got new responsibilities now with this little one. I found a place for your'll to stay. It's a little cottage just off campus here. You can still study, but at your own pace. I'll put money in your accounts for the bills and then you'll have more time for the baby.' Ashok watched Surya's face for signs of an argument. She was like her mother in that respect – stubborn until she got her own way.

'So, you arranged a place for us on this campus. We're not going home?' Surya didn't know why she'd asked that question. Of course, they wouldn't go home. Her mother had disowned her.

'Well, would you even want to go home, after what your mother and Nanima did to you?'

'Surya's mouth was open before she could think to stop it. 'You're right. How could I go home? I would ruin things for Mummy and her precious neighbourhood. I have ruined your name and reputation already. Why are you even here helping me?'

'Because you're my daughter, no matter what. You both ... well all three of your'll are important to me. When I die, your'll will have to carry on my legacy.' The thought made Ashok sad.

'But we're girls. We're supposed to get married and follow another man's name and traditions. Oh, right, well I ruined all of that now, didn't I? But Anjani can still get married unless you want her to stay a spinster forever?'

'I know that one day, even if you don't believe it now, you'll both get married. And leave me and your mother. But your'll will always be my children. I brought your'll up in my house. You'll never forget that and neither will I.' That was the truth.

'How can you accept this child into your family? Mummy refuses to even acknowledge I exist. And here you are, finding us a place to live and giving us money. Why? Are you doing this out of guilt or shame?'

Ashok let out a deep breath. 'Surya, I know you had a rough year last year and now this year too. I know that none of this was your fault. How can I leave you? Your mother knows this. I won't let you struggle here on your own. Enough of this now. Let's find out when you can get discharged.' This was his duty as a father. He knew that and so did Nirmala, deep down in her heart.

The cottage Ashok had arranged was quaint and cosy. In Victorian style, it had high ceilings, low, wide sash windows and beautiful parquet floors. There was a room each for Surya and Anjani, a large living room with a fireplace, an ancient but homely kitchen, and a bathroom that had new fixtures. All in all, it was a dainty place that would ensure their comfort and safety.

Surya and her baby were released two days after the birth. Anjani and her father worked quickly to furnish their new cottage and stock up on baby's toiletries and accessories. For Anjani, moving and furnishing a new home was a personal enjoyment, like a breath of fresh air in her life. She could rearrange furniture and linen and feel like she was living in a new space. This rejuvenated her soul.

By the sixth day after the birth, Ashok had been away from work for as long as he could. It was time he went back to Durban, but not without naming his grandchild. He had grown rather fond of her over the last few days, even changing her nappy once or twice.

'Girls, have we thought of a name for little one? Anjani?' He sensed their sadness, knowing that it was time for him to go home without them.

'Daddy, you were right. There were very few nice names for girls starting with 'D' but I have some options.' Anjani rummaged through her bag for her trusty notebook. 'I thought the shorter and less complicated the name, the easier it would be for the rest of her classmates to pronounce when she starts going to school.'

'You mean to tell me you found out the initial for this baby? From the pundit?' Surya was amazed. 'How did you manage that one without Mummy flipping her top?'

'I asked a different priest,' said Ashok, beaming at Surya. 'She's part of the family. And like Anjani said, she was born on a very holy day – Ganesh Chaturthi – so why shouldn't she be named with the right initial?'

'Because she is not a holy child. Nanima said this was all sinful remember?' Surya couldn't believe her father had gone ahead and spoken to a priest about her illegitimate baby.

'Surya, stop moaning and choose a name!' Anjani was sick of Surya's attitude. She should be grateful that Daddy was here and taking such a great interest in this baby's life. 'Do you like Dhanya, which means thankful or lucky? Or do you think Deepti is nice? It means full of light. And then I found Deeya, which you know means light of the lamp. What do you like, Surya?'

Surya looked down at her child. It had been six days and she still felt nothing for the little girl besides panic and anxiety. She had to admit it was wonderful that her father was here and had done so much for their comfort and security. She'd never expected it from him, given her mother's attitude. And Anjani – as annoying as she was – had accepted this child as part of her life. Surya's tears returned.

'You name her. Here, take her!' Her eyes blurred and she ran out the room.

Anjani held her quietly content niece who looked up at her face with large, chocolate-brown eyes. She was radiant, like a lamp.

'I think that this is a Deeya. Look at her glowing face, Daddy. She's such a good baby. But I think her mummy is having a hard time coping.' Anjani worried that Deeya was too much of a reminder of the rape for Surya. She hadn't taken to her baby like a normal mother would.

'Give it some time. She has to adjust. This is a big change for her. But I hope that your'll will be comfortable now. Hmm ... Deeya. I like it, but spell it with an 'i'. D-i-y-a, so it's four letters long. That would suit this little one.' Ashok was pleased. He had done what he came to do.

'Guess I'll have to keep a close eye on her, huh?' Anjani was pleased with her father's plans for them, but she was tired of see-ing to her sister. She wanted to focus on her studies this year, and her long-distance relationship with Himal, which her father couldn't find out about right now. Maybe not ever.

'This has been hard for you too, looking after her all the time, I know. But like I said, give her time. She's stronger than you think. Anyways, I think it's time I went home now. Your mother

will be worried. Call me if you need anything, anytime, OK?'
Ashok did not want to leave his girls, but it was time for them to
adjust to their new lives.

HEAVENLY SIGNS

Ashok came home to glum faces in Durban. He'd forgotten to phone Nirmala on his return and had gone straight to the office when his flight landed. Her blood pressure had played up while he was away. They had not told him about it, which made him angry. He'd found out from the doctor, whose receptionist called him to confirm medical aid details earlier that afternoon. Before Nirmala could start an argument, Ashok practically ordered her to bed, knowing that she would internally debate the issue the entire night.

The events in her daughter's life were too much for her to bear. Her head ached as she pulled the duvet over her shoulders and closed her eyes.

'Quickly, let's go inside for the aarti!' I'm shouting at Ashok and Ma.

We took so long to get to the temple today, like we were moving at snail's pace. Luckily we made it in time for the evening pooja. The priest is saying his daily mantra. I can smell my favourite agarbathi – sandalwood – and the camphor from the aarti tray is making nice smoke in front of our golden statues – LakshmiMa and Vishnu Bhagwan. It's so peaceful. I'm closing my eyes and joining in the chanting. God bless my family. All the community ladies are watching me praying so nicely.

Now it's finished. I'm pushing my way through these rowdy people so I can bow down before all the statues and take prasad – today there is bananas and burfi that they blessed for all the devotees.

Ooh, that statue of Shiv Bhagwan – he is sitting cross-legged like a yogi doing meditation. And he is painted blue like when he swallowed the poison and saved the world. His third eye is open also. I feel so small standing in front of him like this. I join my hands and bow down by him. He gave us so much blessings and opened our road. Shiv Bhagwan, thank you for all that our family got. Now where's this Ashok and Ma? They not here.

The rain is slowly starting. The sky is a funny colour too – like orange and purple. I'm walking out in the darkness to find these two. Far in the distance there they; I can barely make them out. They walking back to the car.

'Hey, Ma, Ashok, did you bow down by the Shiva statue?'

They are just looking at me like I am talking to two ghosts. They are shaking their heads from side to side.

'But why not? Your'll must do his prayers or your'll won't get the blessings! Why must I tell your'll that!' I'm shouting at them.

They still look like ghosts and no words are coming out their mouths. They carry on walking back to the car. I am very angry now. How can they be so disrespectful at the temple? They disappear in that rain and I'm standing outside the ladies' toilets. All of a sudden, my bladder is full. I have to go to the toilet before we drive home.

I have no shoes on because I was in the temple. This bathroom floor is icy cold. White tiles it has. And there is water everywhere on this floor. I hope it isn't dirty water. I pull my sari up and walk into the first toilet. Sis! It's stinking. The toilet roll paper is stuck inside. Sis!

The next toilet is also like that. I can smell the urine from far. What a filthy place for a temple toilet.

There is a shower with a see-through curtain next to the filthy toilets. Someone is in there showering at this time of the night. Such a dirty place and they are showering here. Sis!

But, this girl has very nice feet. I don't know why I am looking there but I can see her legs and her side and her arms. She has long black hair too. She must be very beautiful. I feel like I know her from somewhere. Wait, I do know who she is. I'm screaming but my voice can't come out. This naked body – it is Surya. She is dead. Arre Raam! Her eyes opened now and she is looking at me. Now her eyes are closed and she falls down on the floor. I'm running. Far away from that bathroom. I mustn't turn around and look back. I must just run one way ...

Nirmala sat up in her bed. Her clothes were wet from her sweat. In the darkness, she realised it was just a dream. But it was so disturbing. She got up to change out of her damp pyjamas.

In the next room, Nanima settled in for a night's rest. But she too did not have a peaceful night.

What a dull morning it is. But what must I do? Have to get up and wake the girls. Every morning same thing. They lazy girls but Anjani is OK. You tickle her toes one time. Then she get up. But Surya. Oh she is a terrible one that child. I have to drag her and force her out of the bed. Nevermind. Today is a big prayer day. Ganesh Chaturthi today. Everyone must wake up and do prayers for Ganeshji. No excuses.

What we got to complain for? Nothing. Ashok's business is all right. This family everybody knows. Some are envious too. Oh yah, we must do prayers for protection. There's too many evil eyes in this community. They just waiting for something bad to happen. All this time, nobody got anything bad to say about our family. They just waiting. Now I'm tickling this child's toes.

'Morning Nanima!' This Anjani always laughing. At least she happy child. She get up in one shot.

Now this Surya beti. I'm shaking her shoulder. She moaning at me. 'Five more minutes, Ma!'

Now I must fight with her for that blanket. I must pull and pull until it comes out. Then she angry with me. But she is awake now. I must make her sit and learn.

'Now listen, mere bache. Today is very special day on Hindu calendar. I explain before that baby Ganeshji was born to Shiv Bhagwan and Parvati Matha many lifetimes ago on this day. Today we must celebrate his birth. So you two must bath, wash hair and put punjabis on. I'm going to wait for you in mandir and we all do pooja, right?'

Like a good girl, Anjani got up and went to bath. She's always got one one questions. But that good. She is learning Hindu Dharma. Very clever she'll become.

'Do we have to do this every year? Is it not enough that we understand the significance and do it once every couple of years? Isn't God all-forgiving? He gave us this time on earth to chill and enjoy, Nanima. Now I want to enjoy my sleep!'

Surya very naughty girl. Too much ghuusa. She not interested in God or religion. Only party and boys for her. But her Nanima mustn't get angry. Not today. Otherwise Ganapati will not bless family.

'Surya, I take out your punjabi. You get up and go in bathroom, OK? Don't make fuss like this, OK?'

Now she more angry because I shout with her. The way she looking at me. She don't say one word. But she is walking to bathroom to go bath. Now I take out her clothes from cupboard. How her mother let her wear such rubbish clothes, I don't know. Look at this – short, short skirt, and this kind tops will fit small child, not for big girl like this. These are not decent Hindu girl clothes. I can't understand why Surya *hate punjabi so much. We all wore punjabi when we were girls. So lovely it was. My father used to buy and bring for all us five sisters.*

Right in the corner I can see one punjabi. It is lovely mint green and cream colour with gold work and bronze embroidery. Now to make Surya put it on. Therewa! Anjani come out in her red velvet and silk punjabi. She so proud of her Indian clothes. No problems with her.

'Are, mere beti, you look like one flim star! OK, now get your sister ready. Make her wear this and your'll come quickly down for pooja.' I kiss my good girl Anjani on her head.

Then I rush to mandir room. So long the girls took. Must be one, two hours.

'Where these bloody granddaughters of mine? I must tell Ashok and Nimmie,' I am shouting. 'How your'll allow this? These girls don't know Hindu dharma, they don't know discipline. What will happen to their children if they carry on like this, huh? They disrespect Gods! I'm tired of telling you this every time. What we going to do with these children? Your'll their parents, your'll have to do something.'

I am breaking my head for nothing. They don' say anything. We are walking to the jhunda flags with brass pot in our hands. The pot got mixed milk and water and tulsi leaf for offering. Ashok is man of house, so he do first. Now I slowly pour milk onto bamboo jhunda. I'm saying my nice mantra. I asking Ganeshji to calm me down and to teach my granddaughters manners and all.

Arre Raam, Surya's brass pot fell down. Milk is running down all over the bricks on driveway. So clumsy she is.

'If you are so tired of harping on about Hindu dharma, why don't you stop forcing us to do this?'

The way she looked at me and her parents badly with hands on her hips. Like one devil. No one saying anything. We just looking at her. This devil child. Rakshasi.

'I am tired of putting up with this life. I think the time has come for me to leave.'

As she speaking, something funny is happening to her shadow. A light coming out of her shadow. Her arms and legs start disappearing. I'm getting such a shock. Now her hands and arms come back. What kind game she is playing with us now?

'You see, Nanima, I am from another world. And I have been here for this family but you've given me no appreciation or respect. You cannot expect me to respect you and your beliefs if you cannot accept me for who I am. So now I am leaving!'

Surya is one shadow now and she floating off the ground. Just like that, she flies up in the black sky and she's gone.

'No, Surya come back. No, you can't leave me!' Anjani's voice is so loud. I never heard her scream like that before.

She's crying. Arre Raam, she is howling like one animal. My ears start paining. She become so angry now.

'Look what you have done! This is your fault. I will never forgive you or listen to anything you say ever again, you hear me!' Anjani is screaming so loud.

Her face go way terrible. The anger come out her body. She start moving. She is performing one dance. I am so proud of her. She studied Bharata Natyam – the most beautiful, oldest Indian dance. But now her feet are banging the floor and the bricks start coming loose from the ground. Even the trees are shaking and the jhundas fall down.

This good girl, my child I knew her from birth is not the same. She is possessed. Her tongue come out her mouth like one demon. She isn't doing one dance. Her feet start bleeding. The floor is covered in her blood now mixing with the milk. She is cursing us. The concrete from the ground is cracking open. Anjani is one side far from us. Arre Raam, now what we gonna do ...

A gasp of air.

Nanima was in her bed but her heart was banging in her chest. She sat up and put her hand against her flannel nightdress. It was moist. This dream was a bad omen.

Nirmala couldn't sleep. She decided to go downstairs to her favourite armchair and read until sleep returned. As she entered the lounge, she found Nanima pacing the floor.

'Ma, what happened? You OK? Why you awake so late?' Nirmala was afraid that Ma's sugar levels were playing up again.

'Nimmie, I had one terrible dream. Something's not right with the girls. I don't know what Surya has gone and done now, but I feel like something bad is going to happen. Some more bad things from that child, eh, I don't know what to do, Nimmie.'

Ma's hands were shaking as Nirmala reached for her arm to sit her down.

'You know Ma, I also had a very bad dream. It was about you and Ashok and I found Surya dead. You're right. This family feels like it is cursed now. What are we going to do?'

'Maybe we should go see that Guruji again. He'll see and tell us if we got some bad thing in this house. Maybe someone was jealous and did something. We can phone his house first thing tomorrow. We can't leave this like this.' Nanima was still perspiring, and wiped her forehead with her handkerchief.

'Maybe you right. I don't know who else to turn to and Ashok is very upset but he won't listen to me if I tell him about Guruji. We'll go on our own. I'll phone him as soon as Ashok leaves the house tomorrow. Let me warm some milk for you now. Then you must go sleep.'

Nirmala hated keeping things from her husband but she knew he wouldn't understand their need to consult someone from a religious point of view. He preferred to handle things on his own. But in her heart, she knew the Guruji could see things and would at least help them calm their minds.

SPIRITUAL INQUISITION

'You are not telling me the whole story. I can't help you if you don't tell me why you so worried about your daughter. What happened that you so worried?'

The holy man was questioning Nirmala. His yellow dhoti was draped over a white shirt. His frown deepened as he asked the questions. The three lines of vibuthi painted across his forehead expelled loose particles of ash as he frowned. His hair, a mixture of grey and black strands with a ponytail at the nape of his neck was covered in vibuthi. He moved his hands around in a large brass tray filled with more of the ashes mixed with cloves.

They were sitting in his prayer room – a large shed outside his house. Nirmala and Nanima had waited for twenty minutes and moved from plastic chair to plastic chair outside the shed until they could finally have their time with the Guruji. His assistant, an elderly lady dressed in a white sari and grey jersey, ushered them in. Her shifty eyes always made Nirmala nervous. What if she told the whole neighbourhood about everyone's problems? But the Guruji was good like that, so Nirmala kept coming back for his guidance.

Mrs Naidoo – Durban North's finest self-proclaimed grapevine and Nirmala's curtain-peeking neighbour – had briefly mentioned him some years ago. Mrs Naidoo had since moved on to a Tamil Guru, but Nirmala liked the insight that this Guruji gave them. With his advice, they had prospered. Until now, that is. Now she didn't know what to do. They had told him about their nightmares and that Surya had turned their family upside down.

'Guruji, Surya has done something. She is ... she was ... well, now she is a mother.' Nirmala was deeply embarrassed to say anything about her daughter's illegitimate child.

'How did that happen? Your dreams are very powerful, but I must hear the whole story about Surya first,' he said.

Nirmala explained the story as she knew it. She didn't forget to mention that she thought Surya had brought this trouble into her life and it had affected the whole family.

'So what your'll did when she came home?' asked the Guruji, his frown deepening once more.

'We sent her back. She making too much trouble for mother and father,' Nanima chimed in.

The Guruji glared at Nanima and she cowered in her chair. He lit a large block of camphor and placed it in a clay lamp in the middle of his tray of ashes. He then skilfully placed a handful of cloves on the burning camphor without scorching his fingers. The cloves shot out all around them.

'Hmm,' he said, nodding as he closed his eyes. His lips moved in silence as he mouthed some Sanskrit verses. He took a deep breath and drew a picture of Ganeshji's head and trunk in the tray of ashes.

'What you seeing there, Guruji?' Nirmala asked, afraid of the answer.

He opened his eyes and looked from Nanima to Nirmala. He

handed the tray to his assistant, who quickly packed the ashes into a piece of paper torn from a telephone book. They must go through a number of telephone books judging by how many people sat outside each day.

'You know what day it was two days ago?' he asked them. They nodded. 'Ha, tell me what day it was?'

'Ganesh Chaturthi,' said Nanima triumphantly. 'I fasted whole day.'

'Oh, for who you fasted? Yourself?'

'No, for the whole family. Why you asking me like that?' Nanima didn't like his tone.

'Well, you wasted your time. Both of your'll!' The Guruji banged his hand on the wooden floor.

'Until your'll don't bring your daughter home, you mustn't pray for any deity, understand?' He was very angry with them. It didn't take a connection to God to tell that these two ladies were wrong in their actions.

Nirmala wondered how any Guru could tell a person not to pray. 'But how can we not pray to God? He protects us if we pray to him.'

'Open your eyes. God is very angry with your'll. Ganeshji is the main one who's angry. Why? Because your'll left your child there!' He shook his head. He couldn't understand their abandonment of their own daughter.

'How can you say that? What proof you got?'

'Arre, you came to me, Ma! Your dreams are the proof. You turned your child away. You didn't believe her. Even I know that rape happens all over the place. What kind of family abandons their daughter? I didn't expect that your'll can do such a thing, hah!'

The ladies were quiet. They couldn't believe what they were hearing.

'Until you bring that child home and ask for her forgiveness, Ganeshji will be very angry with your'll and he won't answer your'lls prayers and all. That's what the Devtas are telling your'll. It's clear. Bring your daughter home. Has she had the child yet?'

'Yes, Guruji.' Nirmala tried to comprehend what he was asking her to do. How could she accept the disgrace Surya had brought onto the family? 'Guruji, what will … what will people say? We sent her to study so far away and she came back with … an illegitimate child! You can understand how we feeling.'

'How you feeling? What about how she is feeling? Her mother and Nani left her there. To fend for herself. And who cares what other people think? It's not for them to know your business anyways. Look at your'lls family! That is more important. Not what everyone is going to say! Look here, your'll are the mother figures in your'lls house. Who is going to bring your'lls family together if not the mothers? The spirits have told me that Surya like her name is like the sun. Yes, you told me what a naughty child she was. But her heart is clean. She's had a rough time. And what did your'll do? Your'll made it worse for her. Ganeshji is angry. Look how frightened he made your'll in your'lls dreams. If you don't bring her back home and ask her forgiveness, he will get more angry. I can't help your'll then!'

Could he be right? thought Nirmala. She had trusted his advice before. He wouldn't have made anything up. The turmoil around Surya was destroying her family.

'Thank you Guruji for your advice,' she said.

'Don't just say thank you and do nothing. The spirits are very clear. Even the Matha's spirit is angry. Go and get your child.'

They bowed down at his feet and at the prayer place. They made a cash donation and left in a daze.

Nirmala drove back in silence. Shamed, Nanima was close to tears. When they got into the house, she sat down at the dining-room table.

'Nimmie, what have we done? We hated that child more than loved her. We sinners for doing that.' Nanima reached for her crumpled handkerchief inside her bra and dabbed at her eyes.

'I know, Ma. I'm also so ashamed. We must make it right now. I must speak to Ashok when he comes home.' Nirmala knew she had to come clean with her husband about visiting Guruji. She would wait for his return from Joburg. Then they would get Surya back home. That's where she belonged.

Nanima went to her mandir. She sat there, cross-legged for over an hour, begging forgiveness from all the deities. Surya did not deserve their cruel words or actions.

Nirmala knew that even the Mathas – the mother deities – were upset with her because she represented their form in this household and she had let the whole family down. Her mother was an old woman with old ways. She didn't know any better about the ways of this modern world. In her eyes, Surya was nothing more than a naughty child. But times had changed and she had to face up to that reality. Surya had done her best to speak to them as her elders and they'd kicked her out the house. Would she even consider speaking to them again?

Then Nirmala imagined what the neighbours would say – what Mrs Naidoo would say – if Surya turned up here with a baby, and the old conflict started up in her heart again.

DANGEROUS THOUGHTS

Trapped, alone, shamed, guilty, exhausted and miserable. That was what Surya had felt in the two months since Diya came home. She watched as the baby gurgled and kicked her little legs on her play-mat. She was born as the season was turning into winter, so the living room's fireplace got used a lot more. At least hauling firewood around helped Surya shed some of her pregnancy weight. She could see her waistline again. But it was nothing like its former glory. The first month and a half had been torturous. Diya woke up every three or four hours and demanded to be fed. If it wasn't milk that she wanted, she needed a nappy change. Surya wondered why any sane woman would put herself through the nightmare of child-rearing by choice. How one little person could be so dependent on another was beyond her understanding.

At first she didn't have a clue what Diya wanted. Anjani was more the motherly type. She tried the bottle and Diya was satisfied. Together, they had figured out how to put on the nappy. It all came so naturally to Anjani, who was always calm around Diya. Surya couldn't understand it. Why was she so anxious and tearful all the time? She realised that Diya picked up on her emotions and responded badly to them. That was probably why she was calmer around Anjani. It grated Surya that Anjani was once again the preferred sister.

Sometimes, she thought about leaving them. It would be easy to slip out in the middle of the night. Diya was still waking up every few hours, but Surya could time it carefully and slip out the back door an hour after her feed. She could escape this torment. But where would she go? She was certain that if she abandoned Diya, her father would not be so generous with his monthly allowances. He would give up on her, like she had given up on herself. She wondered what Ashraf was up to. He had kept his distance since Anjani had ordered him around after the rape and the police had questioned him about Surya's car. How she missed that beautiful car. She so badly wanted a joint right now. Just one spliff would calm her down and help her to release the anxiety.

Anjani walked into a quiet house. The lights weren't on but the glow of the fireplace brought light to the living room. Diya was fussing on her play-mat. She cried out as soon as she saw Anjani.

'Hello my baby girl. How are you? Are you lonely, hey? Let's go find your Mama.' Anjani picked her up and cuddled her. Her hands and feet were cold from lying on the floor. Where could Surya have gone?

She walked around the house turning on lights as she went. Surya was not in her room or anywhere else in the house. The back door was ajar.

Surya was lying on the garden swing on the back veranda, fast asleep.

'Hey! Wake up.' Anjani shook her sister's shoulder. Surya woke up with a fright.

'Huh?'

'What are you doing sleeping outside?'

'Uh, I don't know. I must've dozed off for a minute. It's dark already?'

'A minute? Look around you. Yes, it's dark. You left Diya lying on the floor since when? When did you go outside, Surya?'

'I don't know what time it was. It must've been a few minutes ago. And why are you shouting at me? You'll upset Diya.' Surya didn't like being questioned like a little child.

'I'm shouting at you because you left your two-month-old baby on the floor for the afternoon, unattended, while you took a nap outside. Can you see the problem with this? I guess you can't! Let me spell it out for you! Anyone could've walked into this house, picked up Diya and walked out again and you wouldn't have even known it. And you left her in the living room with the fire burning. What if something caught alight? She could've been killed in there. And again, you would've been none the wiser. Why didn't you think about that?'

'Don't you think you're overreacting? Diya is fine. Nothing happened. Take a chill pill.'

'No, Surya. You need to wake up! You have a child now. You can't just behave anyhow and think everything will be OK. You have to think of her needs first. Her safety and comfort. She needs you, remember?'

'No, you remember, Miss Smartypants. You think you know everything. That you're in control. Is this your baby? Well? Is Diya your child? No! She's not. So stop acting like you're her mother. You're not! I am! You got it? And I will take care of her however I feel.'

'Fine, take her. I'm done here!' Anjani handed Diya over to

Surya, stormed out of the kitchen and banged her room door shut.

Diya started to cry. It was a loud wail in Surya's ears. She couldn't take it any more. She sat down at the kitchen table, placed Diya on the table and sobbed with her. Diya stopped crying and looked at her mother. She smiled and put her tiny, podgy hand on Surya's head. Surya looked at her child. Did Diya understand how her mother felt?

Anjani threw her bag on the floor and flopped onto her bed. She was tired of doing everything for Surya. She hadn't asked to be in this situation either, but she was trying to make the best out of a difficult time for Surya and Diya's sakes. It seemed that Surya didn't appreciate any of it. She was so resentful and negative all the time. Anjani needed a change of scenery. Maybe if she weren't here, Surya would bond with Diya. They didn't seem to be comfortable with each other.

She couldn't blame Surya for feeling apprehensive about Diya. Anjani was sure that she reminded her of the rape every time she looked at her. But surely she could see that Diya was an innocent baby who needed her mother's love? Anjani had to admit that she had fallen in love with her the moment they first brought her to Surya. She loved Diya as if she were her own child. There was something magical about the baby that Anjani couldn't quite figure out. There was an angelic glow about her and she was so serene, unlike most babies. Her eyes seemed to speak of other lives or of knowledge beyond their comprehension. Whatever it was, Diya was special and it was their duty to protect her. Surya needed to come around to the fact that she was a mother.

She decided against having supper with Surya. She wasn't that hungry and didn't want another confrontation with her sister. The last two months had been difficult. She'd had to adjust to having a baby in the house and making sure that Surya was coping. Then she'd had to keep up with her lectures and tutorials and assignments. It had been hard work and she felt constantly tired. And then there was Himal. She missed him. He was off somewhere in the Kruger National Park, making a name for himself as a travel photographer. They kept in touch by email and text messages but he was often out of cell phone range.

She pulled up her blanket and imagined his strong hands around her waist, his lips brushing the side of her ear. She was tired. So very tired.

It was a grey day in Durban. It felt like winter but it wasn't cold. She walked into the back garden. Durban winters were never cold; they just weren't as sticky as the summers. Something didn't seem right though. It was too quiet out here. Where was her family? And Amos, their friendly house-help? The back garden looked terrible. There were no flowers in the flowerbeds, just patches of green grass and craters of brown mud. It must have been raining, since there was mud everywhere.

She was standing in that mud now. As children, she and Surya had loved playing with the brown goo after the rains. She looked up into the grey sky. The clouds started swirling and grew darker. Lightning streaked across the sky. Was she about to find herself in an electrical storm?

The corner of her eye caught movement in the cliffs surrounding their garden. Something came out of the mud. She made out a long, curled trunk. There were others. She heard drums. Their beating became louder and faster. As she turned around, seven heads emerged from the fresh earth. Her heart pounded with the drumbeats. She was scared but glued to the ground.

The elephants encircled her, thick mud dripping from their hefty, crusty bodies. She made to move. They trumpeted. She froze again. One of the elephants – a bull – moved towards her. It picked up its front feet and looked at her. Its eyes were gentle and wise. Her fear dissipated. The bull trumpeted and began to dance. It was magnificent to watch such a large animal move so gracefully. Then they all lined up in front of her and bowed as low as elephants could go. Her heart leapt. She bowed back and smiled. She felt blessed to be acknowledged by the elephants.

Anjani woke up with a start. It was early morning. The neon digits of her alarm clock read 3:50am. Her heart was beating hard in her chest. What could her dream have meant? Whenever she had one – which was more often than not – she always tried to understand it based on her feelings. If she felt good after the dream, she knew it foretold good news. So what was she feeling now?

Besides excitement at viewing a dancing elephant, she felt exhilarated by life. She felt that her luck was about to change. But how? If she looked at the symbolism, what did a dancing elephant mean? In Hinduism, the elephant was considered a good luck symbol. She'd seen seven in her dream. There was also Ganesha, the elephant-headed God who represented prosperity and the removal of obstacles.

Statues of a dancing Ganesha had always been sought after in the Hindu community. Nanima used to say that prayers to a dancing Ganesha brought even more good fortune to one's home than prayers to a seated Ganesha idol. Maybe it meant that she should find a dancing Ganesha and keep it in this cottage. She had to admit it had been months since she had prayed wholeheartedly to any of the Hindu deities. Maybe she needed to introduce Diya to Ganeshji since she was born on his auspicious day.

Anjani went back to sleep with this revelation in her mind. She tossed and turned until her alarm rang. After taking a shower, she cleaned out a corner of her room that faced the sun. She placed a bedside table close to the window, and lit an agarbathi that her mother had given her last year. The rose-infused smoke from the incense filled her senses. She placed the only picture she had for prayer next to the incense holder. The images of Lord Ganesha flanked by Mother Lakhsmi, goddess of material and spiritual wealth, and Mother Saraswati, goddess of knowledge and progress, stared back at her, offering their serene blessings. She brought her hands together and said a prayer.

An overwhelming sense of humility washed over her. She knew she had received a sign from the heavens. Their lives could have been so much worse, but instead everything was fine. She just had to convince Surya to see it the same way and perhaps they could visit the mandir off campus so that Diya could have her first visit to God's house.

–

Surya watched Anjani walk away and slam her bedroom door behind her. Now she'd done it. Now everybody had abandoned her. She was left holding this child, who was supposed to bring light into their lives. But all she did was take Surya back to that wooden cabin. She's the light in Anjani's world, thought Surya. Not mine.

After giving Diya her bottle, Surya changed her nappy and put her down to sleep. She'd wake up in a few hours. Probably when Surya was falling asleep. Diya wriggled and fussed in her mother's arms, sensing the irritation. She knew a big part of Surya didn't want her around.

Surya threw herself on her bed. Then it came to her. First in parts, then she put it together. It was hazy but she remembered. He drove away with her in her beautiful red car. He parked in the dark behind some trees. She was laughing at the cold and how few clothes she had on. How stupid she was, she thought.

He started kissing her and touching her all over her thighs. Then he changed his mind. She couldn't see his face clearly. They were driving again. It was so dark. Why didn't he use the lights? She asked him that. He ignored her. The drive was making her tired and she wanted to go home. He ignored her request again. Then they came to that cabin. And she went blank. Why couldn't she remember? Did she want to remember? It was all so fuzzy, but Surya was sure that her memory of that night was coming back to her.

Then she remembered waking up in that spider-infested hole. What was the use of remembering? There was no point. If it was him, he was long gone. She didn't report the rape, so the police were probably not even looking for him over a stolen car. He had ruined her life forever. And she had this child, Diya, to prove it. There was no happily ever after for her. Nobody was going to love her. Yet she was supposed to be grateful for this life and this child.

Diya lay wrapped up in her cot. Her gentle breathing was the only sound Surya heard. She could easily walk out of here. Anjani would come to Diya's rescue. She always did. She would be angry but she'd easily adjust. Maybe she should leave a note for her sister though. After all, she was the only one who had stood by her through this whole mess. Surya sat down and took out a notepad and a pen.

THE ART OF LETTER-WRITING

Behind the marble columns and oversized glass front door of a once happy family abode, Ashok pondered a different thought: when a husband cannot talk to his wife, the entire home is a miserable place. He couldn't stand Nirmala's silent treatment. Even her shouting was better. Without words, he couldn't reason with her, but it was as if she had given up the need to talk to him. How was he supposed to reconcile with that? So he spent more time at the factory. At least he could talk to his employees, even if the conversations were only work-related.

These days, work was all he had to fill his time. There was a certain amount of peace in monotonous tasks like receiving orders and calling suppliers. There was only one way of doing these things and no emotions were involved. Home was full of quiet awkwardness, anything but peaceful. He would try to talk to Nirmala again. Maybe his long absence from home would have given her time to cool off.

A single setting at the dining table awaited Ashok. A bowl of steaming moongh dhal and freshly toasted rotis lay next to the plate. A crisp jeera chilli papad and mango pickle dressed the setting as accompaniments. Nirmala walked in with the final touch – a glass of ice water and lemon. She knew how to satisfy Ashok's dietary needs, especially after a long trip away from home. Perhaps this spread proved that she had missed his company.

'He waved the white flag. 'Moongh dhal – my favourite, Nimmie. Come join me?'

'We've already eaten.' She walked away.

'Nirmala, you gonna have to talk to me sometime. You can't keep ignoring me like this.' Ashok realised too late that his voice was a little too loud. The white flag was on the floor now.

Nirmala stopped at the doorway. 'You ignored me when it came to your daughters. Now we are the laughing stock of the whole community. I can't show my face in public any more. Everybody knows about Surya's pregnancy, thanks to Mrs Naidoo. You know why? 'Cos of your wonderful idea to bring that child of yours here. And now you want to talk?'

She didn't want to hear his response. Maybe it was wrong to speak to your husband like that, but his choices for their children brought all the trouble into their lives. For that, she couldn't forgive and forget. Surya would have got away with it again. Even the Guruji believed that the shame she brought on the family could be excused. How could Nirmala accept that and live with her daughter and her child? Never. It was unacceptable.

The Guruji was wrong. Fresh pain jabbed Nirmala as she remembered the callous words Mrs Naidoo had for her friends. It was so hard to even drive to the markets or the mall. Everyone staring. They all knew the story by now. Mrs Naidoo and her friends would've spread the word about the illegitimate child of the Harsingh family.

Maybe she should talk to Ashok and they could move to a new neighbourhood. Westville was a decent suburb with lots of green trees and smart houses. It had a nice Indian community and it was close enough to the Durban Hindu Temple. Maybe then they could be in peace. That would be it, she thought. The only way she would make peace with Ashok and the girls would be if they moved house. It didn't matter that this was pure manipulation. The hushed gossip and stolen stares at Nirmala's shame were unbearable. If Ashok was truly sorry, he would move for her. New people in a new community wouldn't judge her and her family.

Nanima was rolling soft puri dough in the kitchen. 'You know, Guruji guided you so long. So many years. How can he be wrong now?'

'I know Ma. But still. How can we live here with that rubbish neighbour of ours? See how quickly the whole town knows what happened to Surya. Guruji is wrong this time. I can't put up with this.'

'What you going to do? Maybe we didn't understand what he said properly. Let's go back to him.' Nanima wanted Guruji to see her daughter in this state. She needed spiritual help.

'Yah, maybe we'll go see him again. Tomorrow morning. I'll phone. Otherwise I got another plan.' Nirmala didn't feel like complaining to her mother. Maybe they'd been so upset over the last few months that they'd misunderstood the Guruji.

–

Anjani's eyes scanned the page. This was no apology note. Surya had other plans.

My bestest Anjani,

I know you will take better care of Diya than I ever could. She's not a constant reminder of a sketchy memory for you.

I can't pretend that I'm OK any longer. I must go now. And maybe my actions will make you mad, but Mummy and Nanima will see just how far they've gone.

I love you for everything that you've done for me. Please tell Daddy the same.

But I'm not worth it. Please don't hate me for going.

I'll never be too far from you. I promise.

Love you always and forever,

Surya

She searched Surya's room. Surya's bright blouses and skirts splashed the dark wooden floor with a wash of colour. Her bag was the only thing missing. She was searching for something else as well, but it wasn't there. Anjani stood up. The shock of what she had read was ringing in her ears. Her eyes circled the room. They stopped at Surya's desk spewing books and lecture notes. The drawers. Anjani's ears picked up the sound of Diya rousing from sleep. She ignored it. Stationary in the top drawer. More notes in the middle drawer. Luck was in the bottom drawer. There it lay, next to her identity book. One piece of paper that would allow Anjani to get a move on.

Anjani thought about the words in Surya's note: *Mummy and Nanima will see just how far they've gone.* There was only one place Surya would go to prove something to her family. She had joked about it when they'd read Hansel and Gretel in primary school: 'Mummy, if you ever take me to a forest and leave me there because I'm a naughty girl, I'll find my way back home. I'll show you!' Anjani had a very strong hunch that this was what Surya was intent on doing. She hoped she was right and would get there in time.

With Diya's birth certificate, her ID book, and Surya's note in her hand, Anjani packed her overnight bag and made for the airport. She would call Ashok on the way. Diya looked up at her with expectant brown eyes.

'Don't worry, we're going to get her back, my baby.' Diya smiled as if she understood her aunt's determination.

–

It was strange travelling to the airport with no luggage, but this was the last plane trip so it was bound to be different. Colours everywhere were brilliant. Even the airport tiles shone as the lady cleaning them smiled at Surya. It was as if she knew. Maybe her chunky brown braids and wooden beaded earrings gave her shamanistic abilities. It was hard to smile back. Surya wasn't sure if her lips moved enough to be considered a smile.

'Where's your luggage, ma'am?' asked the taxi-driver.

He held open the passenger door of his beige taxi. His rotund midsection, complete with hairy navel, peeked out from under his worn navy t-shirt, which was a size too small for him. *Welcome to Durban*, she thought.

'I need to go to 155 Ocean View Drive, La Lucia please.' Surya ignored his puzzled look.

The taxi reeked of cigarette smoke mixed with cheap deodorant. Surya wondered what foreign guests thought of tourist services such as this one. She rolled down her window as he drove off, letting the temperate sea air fill her nostrils and blow through her hair one more time. The tropical palm trees and fields of sugar cane gave the trip an idyllic holiday feel. Surya wished for a better destination.

He dropped her off outside Mrs Naidoo's house. The large brick wall concealed her arrival, but Sasha the Dobermann smelt their presence. Patrolling the perimeter, she howled and barked at the gate. Surya handed two fresh R200 notes to the driver and told him to keep the change. He grinned and jumped back into his taxi before she could change her mind. Surya, preoccupied with what lay ahead of her, stared at the marble columns of her parents' home.

It was eight-thirty in the morning. Ashok would have already left for the factory. She just had to wait for Nirmala and Nanima to make their exit. Precisely what time that would happen, she could not predict. Nobody noticed her walk past the front of the mansion. She made her way to the shade of the palm trees far away from Sasha and any other unwanted attention.

She didn't have long to wait before Nirmala's midnight-blue Honda Accord glided out of the driveway. Nirmala and Nanima had the same sullen faces she'd seen the last time she was in Durban. What a waste. So many families put up high concrete walls and electric gates to protect themselves from the criminal elements, but here was a family whose trouble came from within.

All Surya had to do now was wait for Amos or Maria to appear. Soon Maria surfaced from the kitchen door near the back gate. She was holding her favourite yellow enamel mug, steaming with her usual strong black tea, and a thick brown-bread jam sandwich in her other hand. Surya took a moment to watch her family's domestic worker.

Maria had been part of the household since Anjani and Surya were babies. Her strong hands had washed their clothes, their dishes, and the windows for as long as the girls could remember. Maria was always neatly dressed in her lavender overcoat with the little green and white flowers on the frilly borders. Despite all the hard work she did for the family, she still made time in the afternoon to shine her smooth skin with Vaseline petroleum jelly before flashing a smile at Amos. Pity Amos was more interested in Mrs Naidoo's domestic worker, Promise – a much younger, slimmer lady. Maria would make a man very happy if she ever got over Amos.

'Surprise, Maria! I'm home. Where is everyone?'

Startled, Maria spilled some of her tea. '*Au*, Surya. When you come? Madam and Gogo have gone just now, but I am happy to see you.'

'No problem. I'll wait for them here. You want to let me in?' Just like that, Surya found her way into her old home.

PLANNING AND PATIENCE

There was no queue this time, no line of white plastic chairs leading from the garden, with its protruding peepal tree roots, into the small room at the back. All the mandirs in Durban had a peepal tree nearby. It was believed that Lord Vishnu himself was born under a peepal tree, so it was worshipped even without any idols or images of deities.

Everybody was still talking about her disgraceful daughter, thought Nirmala. It was, after all, the first piece of juicy news about the Harsingh family in a long time. Ever, in fact.

Rose agarbathi filled the room with fragrant smoke.

'Oh, Mrs Harsingh. You look so troubled. I take it Surya is back at home?' asked Guruji.

'No. Haven't you heard? The whole of town is talking about it, thanks to my neighbour.' Nirmala couldn't help but feel sorry for herself. Even though Guruji had shouted at her and sent her off the last time, she still felt she could share her grief with him.

'So Surya isn't home.' Guruji stroked his wiry beard and heaved a sigh. 'Tell me why she isn't home yet.'

'Guruji, last time we left here so ashamed. I prayed for Ganeshji's forgiveness. Then I went to the mandir and Mrs

Naidoo was broadcasting to everybody how Surya was pregnant. Now how can I live here when everybody knows what happened in our house?' Tears filled Nirmala's eyes.

Guruji fought back the urge to shout at her again. Perhaps he had been too hard on her the last time. It was true that children presented some of the biggest challenges in life, even for the strongest people.

'Listen, Mrs Harsingh. I told you what your'll need to do last time. Your'lls family has fallen apart. I can sense how upset everyone is. The only way to make it right is to bring that daughter of yours home. What other people say, you can't control it. Leave them. But doesn't mean your'll must do things to please them. Now listen, do what is right for your'lls family. Leave everybody else out of it.' Guruji turned his tray of ashes. The camphor with three cloves was in flames.

Nirmala watched in despair. Guruji didn't want to say any more. He closed his eyes and looked heavenward. The cloves shot out into a corner of the tray. He took those little embers and mixed them with the ashes.

'Keep this with you when you speak to Surya. She'll be angry but she must come home. Ganeshji wants it that way, your'll understand?'

The last part of his sentence made Nirmala feel like she was back at school and he was one of her stern teachers. He placed his ashy thumb on each of their foreheads in blessing. There was nothing more she could say; he didn't want to hear her complaining.

On a normal visit, Nirmala would ask her mother what she thought of his advice. Today she felt defeated. Of course she wanted peace in the home. But the curious looks and gossip from the entire neighbourhood ate at her mind. How do you stop worrying about something staring you in the face every day? She thought about Ashok. Not being able to talk to him was painful. He was only looking after his children's interests. Who was she to judge him? We all pay for our sins eventually. Karma catches up with all of us, even Surya and that miserable hypocrite, Mrs Naidoo.

'I want my family to be back to normal again, Ma,' she said to Nanima. She had to swallow her pride for her family's sake.

'We call Surya then?' Nanima wanted to say sorry to Surya for pushing her out of the house.

'Yes, I think so.'

–

Surya watched as Maria made herself another jam sandwich.

'Thanks Maria. You can go home after you finish your tea. I'll tell Madam when she comes back.' She didn't want any disturbances or any witnesses.

'But I didn't do the ironing yet.' Maria wasn't unhappy to be given the rest of the day off, but she wasn't used to it.

'Don't worry about it. You can finish tomorrow. I'm locking up. See you. And Maria? Look after yourself. You're a first-class lady.'

She half-pushed Maria out the kitchen door, sandwich still in her hand. Now she had to be quick. She slid open the glass doors to the dining room veranda and walked into the back garden. It was beautiful, this space she had known all her life. It was funny how everything seemed so big when you were small. She and Anjani had run around this garden for hours as kids. The space appeared smaller than she remembered, but still inviting. The green lawn glistened with the last drops of morning dew. From the golden heads of marigolds to the raging bougainvillea, everything seemed brighter than usual. The fresh air was intoxicating. Apparently the world took on greater clarity when one planned one's ending.

Surya hurried to the Wendy house, where the ladder would be. She hoped she wouldn't run into Amos, who'd no doubt want to help her carry the ladder inside and enquire about its use. Her hands shook as she unbolted the door. A bolt on a wooden door. It reminded her of *that* wooden door again, and of him. Her rapist. She could only call him that in her mind. Never out loud. Why had he chosen her? What would he say if he knew what she was about to do as a result of his actions? Would he ever pay for what he did to her? Would Diya ever know who he was and how she came into this world? Anjani would tell her. She would be brave enough to tell her the truth, and strong enough to deal with Diya's reactions.

Inside the Wendy house, her eyes caught the reflection of a pink pillar and a childhood memory came flooding back. Anjani was holding her favourite doll – Rajasthani Princess Barbie – with her long, dark-brown hair and red organza gown. Her silky plastic skin was darker than the standard Princess Barbie because she was the Indian version. Surya would miss Anjani the most, but she had to leave this life behind.

With the ladder inside the lounge, Surya locked the sliding doors behind her and drew the net curtains. Now to find a rope. She went upstairs to the old school cupboard in her bedroom. When her bare feet sunk into the plush cream carpet she closed her eyes and allowed her naked toes the pleasure of being in her childhood home one last time. Then her stomach turned into a knot. As much as this was her final exploration of her former comfort zone, she had to get a move on. There was no sense in putting off what needed to be done.

The steel cupboard was covered in her favourite material – one of Nanima's old Banarasi saris, with a heavily embroidered gold border enveloping the shocking pink silk. It was hard to imagine that Nanima had ever worn such bright colours. They had only known her in shades of cream, pale yellow and white. Surya carefully laid the pink sari on her old bed and returned her attention to the inside of her school cupboard. There was a giant canvas rolled up with string. Surya knew exactly what it said in huge, orange letters: *Vote for Surya. We'll go further!*

It sounded so lame now, but in her carefree Grade 11 days everyone had loved her and she'd become class president. Unfortunately, her presidency hadn't lasted the whole year; she'd been busted for having too many extracurricular adventures. If only she could go back in time, she would listen to reason. But it was too late for regrets now.

Surya found her old skipping rope in the recesses of the dark, cold cupboard. That is how they would find her body: they would step into the darkness of their precious home and she would be cold. They would be shocked, but they would move on.

She went downstairs again, this time to her father's den – the TV room. She would miss him so much. Another flashback took over: two little girls dressed in white party dresses and pink stockings with bows in their hair. Ashok was younger and full of energy. His face lit up and his brown eyes grew large as he read out loud to the girls about a princess, a pirate who took her away, and the handsome prince who fought valiantly to rescue her. Their father always made the time to entertain and thrill them to the point where they could hardly sleep at night. What a wonderful father he had been. It wasn't fair to have let him down so badly; he would be better off without a worthless daughter who caused him nothing but endless trouble.

All that was left to end this misery was a pair of scissors. Surya walked into the kitchen. A faint spicy smell lingered in the air: coriander, green chillies and roasted peanuts. Her mother's famous nut chutney. A good plate of broad-beans curry was not complete without a generous helping of nut chutney to add bite to the creaminess of the beans. Her stomach reminded her that she hadn't eaten anything in the last day but hunger no longer mattered. Her mother's food was delicious but Surya believed it was given to her with a callous heart. Nirmala loved harbouring grudges. She had been angry with Surya for as long as she could remember. She didn't want to repeat the cycle of hatred with Diya; one more reason to leave them all behind.

Surya's legs almost betrayed her as she mounted the ladder in the entrance hall.

–

'Daddy, hi! I was trying to call you hours ago but your phone was switched off! Where are you now?' Anjani's voice sounded frantic. Ashok heard Diya fussing in the background of some noisy place.

'Hello, sweetie. I'm at the factory. Where are you?' Then he heard the *bing bong* of an announcement. 'You're at the airport?'

'Daddy, come quick. Come fetch me. I'm in Durban airport. You have to hurry. Surya has lost it this time. I'm waiting for you outside. Come quickly now, please.' Anjani rang off. He had never heard his usually level-headed daughter sound so panicked before.

Ashok was normally a cautious driver, but today he felt the power under his right foot as he pressed the accelerator of his SUV. Whatever Surya or Anjani had done, he had to sort it out. Ten minutes later, the SUV roared into the airport pick-up zone.

He spotted Anjani waving frantically with Diya in her arms, but no luggage. With his hazard lights on, Ashok reached over and opened the passenger door. Diya gurgled and smiled as Anjani climbed into the car, blissfully unaware of the drama unfolding in her family.

'Drive, Daddy. We must get home before she has time to do it.' Anjani's voice was panicked.

'Do what Anjani?' Ashok was scared to hear the answer.

'Take her life. Go. Drive.'

Neither of them said another word.

DISTURBANCES

His elephant trunk curled in thought as Ganesha watched the young soul's ego and body attempt to tarnish itself. This was not what he had intended. He needed the assistance of an older soul.

'It is already written, Putr. Watch fate unfold without fear.' Mother Parvati placed a reassuring hand on her elephant-headed son's shoulder.

–

Nirmala unlocked the front door and let Nanima walk in first as she usually did. Then she turned and latched the door from the inside.

'Arre Surya? You here?' Nanima's words stopped Nirmala's hands in surprise.

'Surya! How did you know to come?' She was thrilled. This time there would be no turning her down. Then Nirmala saw the ladder and looked at Surya's defeated face. 'Surya? What is this? What you doing up there?' Nirmala had a horrible feeling she knew the answers to her questions.

'So you caught me. It was supposed to be a surprise you

know.' Surya's anger surged on seeing the two women who had disowned her.

'That's not funny. Now get down from there and give me a hug. I want you and Diya to come home, where you belong.' Nirmala meant it.

'How dare you say her name? How dare you? You, who hated me my whole life. I was never good enough for anything. You always had to put me right. Well you are getting your wish today. I am going for good this time. Your shameful, disgraceful child will be out of your life forever!' Surya made sure the noose was tied tight. Her hands trembled from raw emotion.

'No Surya. You don't have to do this. I know you made mistakes in the past. I forgive you. For everything. And I'm sorry for my actions. Now please come down from there. We want you home for good.' Nirmala didn't think Surya was serious about killing herself. This child loved drama. She should have been an actress.

'Oh, so now you forgive me and you think I'll just accept your stupid sorry? I don't want a mother like you. You've been a bitch to me my whole life. Why would I want to stick around and wait for the next time you have a change of heart? Then you will hate me again. No thanks, Mother. Mother? I can't even call you that. You've been a terrible mother to me. But don't you worry. You won't even have to remember me after this. You can live a shame-free life when I'm gone.' Surya knew her mother would remember this every time she walked into the house.

'Arre baccha,' Nanima interjected. 'You mustn't be angry like this. And you mustn't talk like that to Mummy. She is sorry. I am sorry also. Come down from there.'

'Oh don't get me started on you. You brought her up to hate

me. It all started with you, sweet Nanima. I don't know why you hated me so much. Why you couldn't accept me for who I was? I wasn't like Anjani. Not everybody is the same. But you didn't care because I didn't want to sit in your prayer room the whole day! Never mind. I'm outta here.' Surya made her way down two rungs on the ladder. She blinked to clear the black spots that were forming in front of her eyes.

'Carry on, Surya. Blame us for everything. Look what happened to you. Did I ask that man to rape you? Did I ask you to become pregnant with your child? You can blame us all you want. You can hate us also, but we didn't choose to do what you did. You did that. If you think you getting revenge on us, carry on. The only person you are hurting is yourself and your child. If you do this, you will be just like me. Choosing the easy way out. You are after all my child.'

'Oh don't play reverse psychology with me. You made me what I am today. A failure. Because you didn't let me believe that I could do anything right. Yes, I made mistakes, but I didn't ask to be raped either. It wasn't my choice. How dare you think that I chose that to happen to me? It shows how much you hate me.' Surya sat down on the ladder. This was the last time her mother would make her cry. She let it all out in loud wails.

The door flew open, the double-glazed glass threatening to crack as it banged against the wall. Surya stopped short. Ashok lunged forward, Anjani following him with Diya in her arms.

'Surya, please don't do this. For God's sake, please!' Ashok brought his hands together.

'There you come to her rescue again. Like the wonderful father that you are. If only you were such a dedicated husband also. But never mind. I've been telling her to come down from there for the last ten minutes. She won't listen to me. She's busy blaming me for what happened to her. Can you believe it?' Nirmala's words flew out her mouth before she realised how they sounded. She bit her lip in embarrassment.

'Yes, I can believe it. This has gone on for far too long. Yes, I love my children. Maybe too much for you, Nimmie. And it's my fault. I let things come to this. But no more now. Surya, I am putting my foot down in this house today. You will come down from there and you will stay here. I think your mother has realised how wrong she was to send you away. I don't blame you for anything that has happened to you. Look at this child. Look at Diya. It won't be fair to leave her with no parents at all. And it won't be fair to leave your family, especially your sister. You can't give her the responsibility of looking after your child. Please. I'm begging you. Think about what you are doing.' Ashok felt his words were strong.

'Surya, we're here for you. We're not perfect but we're your family.' Anjani was tired and her voice was weak as she pleaded with her twin. 'I don't think I can live without you. Diya won't be able to live without you either.'

Ashok edged closer to the ladder. There was no way he was going to let his daughter slip out of his life over a family feud.

'No, Daddy, don't come closer. I swear I'll put this rope round my neck.' Tears rolled down Surya's face. When last had she had a proper night's sleep? Her head swam as dizziness threatened to overwhelm her. She glared at her mother and Nanima. 'They hate me. I know you love me. And Anjani. And maybe Diya. I'm not a good mother, but then I learnt from the best.'

'Oh, Surya. If you just give me a chance. Listen, today I was going to call you. Today I was going to tell you that I was wrong and that you should come home. Don't you think I'm tired of your father and Anjani being upset with me? Even Guruji and Ganeshji is angry with me!' Nirmala threw up her arms. She felt relief at admitting her flaws. 'I admit it; I can't handle the shame when I walk outside this house. Maybe … maybe you can help me deal with that. When you are here. At home. I'm sorry. I am. For everything I did wrong your whole life. I am the bad mother, not you.'

Nirmala had silenced the room. As everyone stared at Surya, her eyes rolled back in her head and she slumped onto the floor, her body bumping against the ladder on the way down.

'Surya? Surya?' Anjani shook her twin. She felt her pulse. It was faint but definitely there. 'Quick, get some water!' Anjani put Diya down next to her mother. Her chubby little hand played with her Surya's tousled hair.

The grass in this garden was glowing green. Surya remembered the last time she was here and looked around for the little girl. She walked around the garden until she reached a tall, broad tree. Its leaves were blowing gently in the warm breeze. Surya inhaled the refreshing eucalyptus scent. She released her breath as a glint of gingery-brown hair caught her eye. The little angel was clutching a shaggy teddy bear. Her pink silk ribbon hung off her ponytail.

'There you are. How are you little one?' offered Surya.

The angel turned around. What Surya saw shocked her and she took a step back. The little angel's glow was not as bright as the last time they'd met. Her eyes had dark blue rings around them, as if she had aged beyond her years. She did not greet or smile at Surya.

'You didn't keep your promise,' she mumbled.

'But I'm here. What do you mean, my angel?'

'No! You lied to me. You want to leave me!' The angel shoved her with surprising strength.

Surya landed on the grass. She felt too weak to stand up again. She still didn't understand but she had to make the angel happy again. Using her hands, she crawled into a sitting position, fearing her legs were not strong enough to carry her full weight.

'Come now, my little one. I'm here aren't I? What must I do to make you happy and glowing?' Surya hoped she wouldn't be shoved again by this mighty force in a child's body.

'It's simple. Keep your promise.' Her little finger wagged in front of Surya's face as her voice turned into an echo. Then her body disappeared along with her voice.

'No wait, please. What promise?'

Her head pounded. She opened her eyes and looked into a familiar face. Anjani was holding her hand, looking worried as she placed a cold palm on Surya's forehead.

'Surya? Can you hear me? I think she's come to. Quick, the glass of water.'

Words and thoughts swarmed around Surya's head. She remembered her confusion about the promise. She still had to figure out what promise the little angel had asked her to keep.

'Anjani, what promise was I supposed to keep?' Nobody could give her a better answer than Anjani.

'What are you talking about? What promise? Just promise me you'll stop this nonsense idea you have of ending your life!'

'You know the promise. You know. The one to the little angel. I saw her again. Just now. Where is she? I want her to come back.'

Anjani did not respond. She sat back in silence, still holding Surya's hand. Then Surya saw a face appear at her sister's elbow.

Diya broke the silence, responding to her mother's gaze with a tender coo. Surya smiled at her child through her tears. She longed to hold her again and touch her soft, warm skin. The longing seemed to grow inside her one vertebra at a time until she sat up. Diya's little arms reached out automatically for her mother as Anjani moved out of the way of their reunion. Surya embraced her cooing baby with real love for the first time. She met Anjani's eyes. Both sisters knew what this meant. Diya – their light of the lamp – was destined to be with them.

'Can I?' It was Nirmala's first proper look at her granddaughter as she stretched out her hands to hold her. Tears filled her eyes as Diya's met hers. She embraced Surya, physically and with all her heart.

'I'm so sorry, my child. I've been a bad mother. I've been so angry for so long that I forgot to love you. But no more. I want to welcome you to this house again. Whether you finish your degree at Rhodes first or come straight back home, I love you and I want you with me. Please.'

Surya, too overcome with emotion to speak, simply nodded as she held Nirmala. All she wanted was to savour the motherly love she'd been missing for so long.

A SURVIVOR IS BORN

Her relationship with her mother and grandmother was on the mend. Surya could move forward with confidence, knowing that whatever she pursued in her future, she had her family's support. It was her sister's love and spiritual insights that got her through the darkest times. It was her father's compassion and love that got both twins to finish university in spite of all the mental and emotional suffering. It proved that there was still good in people, especially family.

As for the man who forced himself into her life, the coward who thought he took her power: he didn't. How could he be called a man? He was a weak piece of scum, lower than the basest animal form. And she still had enough evidence to make him pay. Whether the justice system would ever find him and bring him to trial, Surya had her doubts, but she needed to end this chapter for her own sake and Diya's. Happiness had been a forgotten emotion for the last three years, but when she exited the door at the Legal Resource Centre building she realised that Anjani had been right: the only way to move forward was to take control again. The first step in the process had been to report the rape – and to do it on her own.

A sense of pride and relief washed over her. The thought of talking about the rape to strangers filled her with dread for a long time, but the staff at the Legal Resource and Counselling centres were willing to hear her story without judgement. They showed her how to make her statement and how to get the university involved in the police investigation. For the first time in a long time, she stood up for herself without Anjani or her father attempting to rescue or comfort her. Perhaps one day, with time, a semblance of peace would return to her life. Until then, she wanted the voices of women to be heard and she would make sure she played her part in that mission.

—

As the official speakers concluded and the launch ceremony came to a close, Anjani couldn't help looking back on that night with a sense of wonder. A conversation with her mother about letting go of shame had prompted Surya to start the Survivor's Foundation to help other women deal with rape and raise awareness of date rape. Her event-planning skills had proved invaluable in this regard. These days, Nirmala held her head high in La Lucia and swelled with pride whenever she spoke about Surya's achievements.

The sisters had come a long way together. They walked hand-in-hand in their stylish cocktail dresses, unaware of the breathtaking picture they made. No longer naïve young girls at university, they were now newly graduated women of courage.

He watched Anjani carry herself confidently across the room, hoping she would not be too surprised at his gesture. She was beaming at Surya as they shared a joke when she stumbled over something and looked down. Anjani picked up the bouquet of passion-pink roses and searched for the card. He couldn't see her face clearly but it was time to move in closer.

It's been a while since I last saw your dimple, Anjani read. *Maybe we can go out sometime? Turn around now!* She knew only one person who wrote such bad notes. She turned around and looked into familiar brown eyes. Himal was smiling back at her, dressed in a charcoal tailored suit. She reached out to him and didn't want to let go. He was warm and welcoming.

His work had taken him to remote locations and it had been two years since she'd last seen him. All her feelings rushed back as if giving her new breath. They had kept in touch over e-mail but she'd thought it best that they concentrated on their new lives. Her studies had taken a dip during her first two years at Rhodes, and he'd been building his career as a photographer. She had followed his rise in photojournalism and watched as his photo features became more prominent in travel magazines and websites. His award-winning work had kept him busy travelling across the country and the continent. But here he was standing in front of her and she didn't know what to say to him.

'Hello, my lady. Are you surprised to see me?' Himal took her hand and led her to her table. She still didn't have words for him as she sat back in her chair. 'I'll take that as a yes then?' He was as charming as ever.

God, he was so irresistible. But something was gnawing at the back of her mind: what was the real state of this long-distance relationship? Could it even be called a relationship? Sure, they'd kept in touch, but not in an intense way.

'Let me not disturb your sister's special moment,' Himal said, turning towards Surya. 'I just wanted to surprise you and say hi.

We can catch up later.'

'Oh no, no, this is one reunion Anjani's been waiting a long time for! Please stay and have supper with her. I have to mingle with my guests anyway.' Surya flashed a smirk at Anjani before leaving the two of them alone.

Himal was beaming, glad to eat dinner in the company of the woman he'd longed for over the last few years. All the travelling he'd done had broadened his mind but his heart always came back to the person sitting in front of him. But she was not her usual bubbly self.

'I know I haven't been in touch for a long time, Anjani. Are you angry with me? I'm sorry. I was out of cell phone range most of the time, and I know that's a bad excuse, but I haven't stopped thinking about you and wondering how you are doing.' He hated that he was babbling.

'It's not that. I know how you work. I've had a lot to deal with here at home anyways. But I thought about you a lot. I've been following your work. You're really talented.'

'So, if you're not angry with me, it can only mean that there's someone else in the picture?'

'No. There isn't anyone else. Himal … I'm just going to come out and say this. What are we doing here? I mean, are we together or not? Are we friends or do you want more? I know I want more, but I don't know about you …'

'You know, being away from home and you for so long has made me learn more about myself and what I want. Anjani, it's you. There's no doubt in my mind. I know that … I love you.' He touched her hand.

Anjani stood up. Himal followed suit. He was afraid that she was going to walk out and leave him hanging.

'What took you so long? I love you too!' She put her arms around him and her mouth searched for his lips.

Their kiss roused the audience, who clapped and cheered them on. No doubt it was Surya who encouraged the raucous applause. Both red in the face, Himal and Anjani sheepishly sat back down at their table.

Surya realised that this was the first time she had ever witnessed her sister display affection for the opposite sex. Her heart strings tugged for a moment as Anjani's dream came true. They had dealt with more than their fair share of drama as a family. She had been so busy with Diya, her studies, and reconnecting with the family that Anjani's heartache had been overlooked. She was glad that longing and doubt ended today. All in all, life seemed like a celebration these days. They had so much to be grateful for. Diya had sealed their happy fate and was truly a blessing in disguise.

Anjani had never felt so light and free in her heart, but there was that gnawing worry again. It was time to come clean with the folks. After everything that the family had been through with Surya, how would she break the news of her relationship with a Gujerati boy to them?

'Himal, I have to tell my family about us. I don't know how they are going to react. You know how strict they are with us, especially about boys. They aren't going to be happy with me bringing home a Gujerati boy. No offence, you know how it is.' But Anjani feared that he didn't know how it was – not really.

His family was much more liberal than hers. He once told her that the only thing his mum had specified about his choice of life partner was that she should be a decent Indian girl. It was as simple as that. Her family, on the other hand, would go into the complications of opening the famous priest's astrological book and finding out if the stars corresponded for the match. Many of her older cousins' matches were turned down because of such astrological enquiries. There was also the issue of finding employment. Anjani had ended up majoring in environmental science and she was eager to put her knowledge into practice. She had a ton of research to do about her job market.

'Well, I guess we have time. Unfortunately I have one last three-month assignment out in the Okavango before I can return home for good. Then I would like to meet your family, if they'll let me.'

They both decided to enjoy the evening rather than focus on their pending problems. For the first time in her life, Anjani experienced the value of a slow-dance with a partner who had openly pronounced his love. They lost themselves in one love song after the next and one tender kiss after another, until the DJ closed the dance floor. Neither wanted the night to end.

'I hope this is officially the last goodbye,' Anjani whispered.

'Don't worry. I'll see you soon. Maybe sooner than you think.' Himal kissed her again.

QUESTIONING GODS AND
CONSPIRING MEN

'She is about to enter the next phase of earthly life. What a sublime soul, Putr.' Mother Parvati watched Anjani playing with Diya.

They had just returned from a visit to Lord Varuna. Ganesha was seated once more with his golden quill in hand. Mushaka nibbled on crumbs of laddoo.

'Yes Matha. Her dues will be suitably rewarded. She has your energy coursing through her earthly form and it shines bright in her actions.'

Mother Parvati peered over Ganesha's shoulder and into his sacred writing.

'Why set more tribulations for her? Has she not endured enough?' She wondered if the next test would dampen Anjani's bright energy.

'O Matha, do you doubt your own strength? She is part of that strength. Do not fear for her. She is wise beyond her earthly appearance.' Ganesha smiled knowingly at his mother.

'May her prayers be swiftly answered, Putr. Om Namah Shivaya.' Mother Parvati was reassured and ascended to Lord Shiva's abode.

—

He put down the empty cup, stained from his third round of coffee. His fingers ran through his grizzled curls once more.

'OK I won't say anything to her but you better not be playing games with me.' The wheels on his office chair squeaked against his weight as he reclined.

'No sir, I promise you, this is no game. I'm deadly serious. It's all been arranged. I just need a little more time to finalise it. Then we can go ahead with the plans. That is if … if you're happy, sir.' He noticed his hands were shaking and quickly placed them on his lap. He had asked. It was done now. He sat up straight in the chair and looked steadily at the man who held his fate in his hands.

'I suppose I owe you my thanks for what you've done for my children. But I want to hear from them first, you see.'

'Of course, sir. I'll check in every week and wait to hear from you.' He stood up, hoping to end the nerve-wracking meeting.

'Right, OK. Keep in contact.' He shook the young man's hand, studying his eyes for signs of deceit. He found none.

THE SMELL OF PROPOSALS

They sat quietly in the lounge, inhaling the miasma of his cologne. Soon the sneezing would begin. Nanima was first. Then Nirmala, followed by Ashok. Surya stood up before she could join in the sneeze fest, making the most believable excuse she could come up with – it was time to give Diya a snack.

'Yes, yes, Surya. Go and get your sister and tell her to come downstairs now.' Nirmala held Surya by her arm before she could escape. 'And put her in a nice punjabi, OK?' she added in a whisper before pushing Surya upstairs.

'Yes Mummyji!' Surya's laugh was bursting to leave her body and it broke free in Anjani's room. 'Jenny, you are not going to believe this. Mummy has outdone herself this time.'

'What has she done now?' Anjani was searching for something, tossing her silk scarves to the floor.

'You don't know who's downstairs? You mean she didn't tell you? Oh my God, the plot thickens!' Anjani looked curiously at Surya. 'My dear sister Jenny, there is someone downstairs who wants to meet you. Mummy's orders are for you to dress in your finest Indian attire and present yourself at once.' Surya almost felt sorry for her sister. First Himal had apparently disappeared off the face of the earth, and now this.

'Now what are you on about? Why must I get dressed? Is she dragging me off to another wedding? At the last one, we weren't even related to the wedding parties. Honestly, this mother of ours is nuts!' Anjani popped her head out of her cupboard. 'And who is waiting downstairs?'

Surya did not want to fight with her sister. She picked out a teal and beige punjabi encrusted with gold embroidery and sequins.

'Here, put this on and meet me downstairs. Unless you want Mummy to come up and drag you down herself?' Surya closed the door with Diya giggling in her arms.

Anjani ignored her sister's commands and pulled out her memory box. She lifted the purple velvet lid. Himal's handsome face smiled back at her. The lights seemed to dance in his eyes even on paper. But why hadn't he contacted her all these weeks?

'Anjani darling? Are you ready?' Her mother disturbed her thoughts.

Anjani shoved the lid back on her memory box and pushed it into her cupboard. She put on the punjabi with Himal on her mind.

–

'So what's going on now, Mummy?' Anjani hopped on one leg trying to put on her sandals. She looked up to find the lounge full of strange faces.

There was a middle-aged lady dressed in a red and gold sari with an oversized handbag on her lap. She studied Anjani from top to toe. Seated next to her was an older lady in a colourful orange and black elephant-print maxi. She had short white hair and could not stop smiling; a slit of gold in her tooth gleamed in the afternoon sun. She was nodding her head in approval but said nothing.

To her left sat the last stranger. He was tall and awkward, dressed in black pinstripe pants and a blue shirt with white cuffs. He couldn't seem to decide whether to sit up straight or settle back into the sofa. His hair was gelled into submission, with a few misbehaving strands that stood straight up. He smiled when he caught Anjani's gaze. What on earth was that smell, though? She looked around for the source of the eye-watering scent.

'Mrs Harry, this is my daughter, Anjani. Anjani, this is Mrs Harry and her mother. And this is her son Raj. He is an engineer and he's working by the airport. Say hello, Anjani.' Nirmala hoped her daughter would be open to this idea. She wasn't getting any younger.

'He-hello. Namaste, Ma. Hello, Raj.' Anjani smiled in greeting but she was boiling inside. Her mother had failed to mention these kinds of visitors.

'So what the girl studied? So far your'll sent her to study. How your'll did that? My Raj didn't want to leave me and my cooking and all; you know how these boys are.' Mrs Harry laughed and the rolls on her half-exposed belly jiggled with her.

Mistake number one, thought Anjani. The woman talked about her as though she wasn't even in the room. And why had her mother not discussed these matchmaking plans with her? Could it be that her father supported this proposal? Was she the only one in the room who was clueless?

Surya sat next to Nanima with Diya on her lap. She watched her sister's expression change from surprise to disgust. Mummy had obviously not discussed the arrival of prospective future husbands and mothers-in-law from hell. It was time for Surya to rescue Anjani for a change. She placed Diya in Nanima's arms and went to her sister.

'Please excuse us for a minute.' She smiled at her mother's guests. 'Come with me Jenny, let's go upstairs now.' She touched her sister's arm and led her away. Anjani did not resist.

–

'That boy was such a nice match for Anjani and from such a nice family also,' Nirmala protested later. 'I'm only looking for a good home for her so she can settle down, you know.' Ashok had just seen the Harry family out the front door.

'A good home for me? Like I'm a dog up for adoption? And did you see how that woman talked about me like I wasn't even in the room? How is that a good home for me, Mummy? And don't tell me you support this, Daddy, really.'

'Oh please Anjani not now! Haven't we fought enough these past years? I knew you wouldn't let me arrange this proposal if I spoke to you first but can't you see I'm doing this for you? You are the right age for engagement now. Nobody is saying you must get married tomorrow. What's the harm in you meeting a few nice boys?' Nirmala sat down.

'Daddy, say something!' Anjani appealed to her father, certain he would disapprove of the arrangements.

'You know what Anjani, you're right. This Raj wasn't right for you.' Ashok reopened the front door, sniffing the air in disapproval of Raj's cologne.

'Thank you for seeing sense.' Anjani sat down in her relief.

'No, but your Mummy is right. I know you just got home from Rhodes, but perhaps you need to meet someone new. Someone who we both approve of.' Ashok glared at Nirmala. 'There is a boy I have in mind that is interested in meeting you.'

'What? Who is it, Ashok?' Nirmala quickly forgot the botched proposal.

'You can't be serious, Daddy! It's like you both want to get rid of me. I mean, honestly Mummy, how could you think that that guy was a good future husband for me? Because he is an engineer? Really? Mr Cologne and Gel?'

The conversation was broken by the sound of Diya's gurgling giggle. Surya looked at her daughter and then at her sister and parents. She let loose her laughter. 'I'm so sorry. Mr Cologne and Gel! Anjani, you kill me.'

The tension was broken. Anjani forgot her anger and Ashok joined in the laughter. Even Nanima giggled a little until Nirmala glared at her. The twins' mother was not impressed with her family this evening.

DANCE TO THE BEAT OF
YOUR OWN DOLAK

The bells jingled on her pink and rose-gold bangles. She was starting to feel more and more like an obedient but frustrated puppy. Her mother was right though and Anjani could not bear to disappoint her father after the stress of their university lives. Still, she thought it odd that he had chosen a proposal for her. She was sure he'd wanted his daughters home with him for at least a few more years before marriage came up.

The mirror defied her mood. She dutifully made the effort for this meeting of families and looked suitably cultured in her blush-pink sharara. At least this time she knew what was about to take place in the living room. She descended the stairs to strange voices and expected politeness amidst the mothers. She looked at the back of the guy's head. He had gingery brown hair and something about the back of that neck seemed familiar.

He turned to stand up and greet her. She stared into a charming face with a charismatic smile and twinkling brown eyes. It was *him*.

'Himal?' Anjani gasped. 'What are you doing here?'

'Hello, Anjani.' Himal could hardly restrain himself from

planting a kiss on her rosy lips. 'I know I have some explaining to do.'

'It's OK, Himal. Let me tell her.' Ashok wanted his family to understand his arrangements. 'Himal met me a few months ago and told me all about your relationship. Of course, I wasn't happy because you didn't say anything to me. But then I heard about his support for you when you tried to find Surya. I knew I could trust him with your future when he told me he wanted to marry you.'

'Wait, Ashok, we never even discussed this. What am I going to tell our families?' Nirmala could feel her blood pressure rise. How could Ashok not consult her about this Gujerati boy becoming her son-in-law?

'You will tell them about this brave young man who stood up to me. You will also tell them about the new project he is launching so that Anjani can put her degree in environmental science into practice. His project has been confirmed and that is why we are all here today. Nimmie, they are about to start the next chapter of their lives. We must prepare for a wedding. That is, if Anjani is happy. Anjani?'

'I cannot believe the two of you conspired behind my back. I lost all hope. But I'm … I'm more than happy.' Anjani turned to Himal and put her arms around his shoulders. She quickly released her hold, remembering that she was in her parents' home.

'Then it's settled,' laughed Ashok. He knew this was the right choice for his daughter judging by their reactions to one another. It was going to be difficult to watch Anjani leave but she was a young woman now and he was so proud of both of his daughters.

–

Anjani had secretly been dreaming of this day since she was a teenager. Despite the fact that she'd grown up in South Africa, these last few days at home represented the return to her Indian roots. Surya had taken a special delight in celebrating this marriage ceremony. She had read out the traditions to Anjani weeks before the big days arrived.

"'In true North Indian tradition, the mendhi night takes place two days before the wedding day. It's a night of bridal beautification and glamour. The grandmothers claim that once the patterns of hardened black paste fall off the bride-to-be's hands and feet, the intensity of the red colour of the henna represents the intensity of the love of the groom for his new bride.' Oh Jenny, your mendhi will come out so dark on your light skin!'

But Anjani didn't care about that. She could hardly believe the events leading up to her wedding. Nirmala had continued to protest about the 'different kind' boy that she didn't want for her daughter, but Himal, oblivious to her apparent discomfort around him, had showered Nirmala with affection. He'd won her over in the end and now they were getting ready for full-scale wedding fever.

Anjani sat in her room staring at the golden threads and beads of her mendhi sharara. She listened to the latest Indian love songs from Bollywood that were blaring on loudspeakers outside. Everyone awaited her entrance onto the stage. The Pakistani mendhi artist would arrive any moment now to begin painting her feet. Being in the spotlight made Anjani uncomfortable but she wanted to enjoy her celebrations.

The mendhi night ensured that Anjani glowed on the stage in her parent's garden in spite of her shyness. The music played, highlighting the festivities of painting the skin black with henna to reveal the scarlet hands and feet of the beautiful bride to be.

'No wonder all the TV adverts portray us Indian people in our best saris, chunky jewellery and ghararas. It's our weddings that give us that reputation!' Surya exclaimed. Despite her lack of interest in Indian traditions throughout their lives, she now revelled in her sister's wedding celebrations.

–

'Are you ready Anjani?' Surya burst into the room beaming from ear to ear. The cars are decorated, the camera man is outside and we're good to go!'

The wedding day had arrived and Anjani had made it through each prayer, hundreds of relatives, and what seemed like hundreds more traditions. All the while her nervousness grew a life of its own. She wondered if Himal would have second thoughts about marrying into her crazy family. And would Surya and Diya be OK when she left home? Waves of sadness were threatening to overcome her. Surya was more excited about the wedding than Anjani could be.

'Oh come on, cheer up, Jenny. It's not like the old days of India where once you got married, we'd never see you again. I know Himal will be happy for you to visit us whenever you wish!' Surya plonked herself on the bed, disrupting the rows of red glass bangles that Anjani still had to put on.

Anjani didn't have the heart to shout at her as she usually did and when she turned her tear-filled face towards her twin, Surya's smile quickly disappeared.

'OK, I'm sorry for teasing. Of course I'll miss you the most.

Who else am I going to fight with? Diya's not much of a talker, you know!'

The thought of Diya brought a smile to Anjani's face amid all the tears. The baby had flourished since she'd arrived in Durban. Despite their initial hesitance around her, Nanima and Nirmala hardly took their eyes off their enchanting granddaughter. They were spellbound. The wedding served as a grand parade for them to show her off and Diya loved all the attention.

'My darling little Jenny,' said Surya. 'You've been my rock for so many years now. Of all the people in this house, you're the one I will miss the most! But look at us. We're all grown up now. I have Diya in my life. And I'll always be close to you. But this marriage, it will be good for you. You'll see. It's time you lived your life. Not mine.' It was Surya's turn to cry. She dabbed the corners of her eyes so as not to mess up her spectacular application of double-volume mascara. Then she hugged her twin and told her that she looked as bad as she did on the day she was born.

Anjani laughed. Surya's teasing was exactly what she needed to help her get over her attack of nerves. She slipped on her red bangles and knew that today was the beginning of the rest of her life.

TWO HEARTS BEAT AS ONE

The cars pulled into the foyer of the wedding venue, hooters blaring to announce the arrival of the bride. Ashok was not one to flash his wealth but this was his daughter's wedding day, so the Harsingh family arrived in a white stretch limousine. Anjani was quickly escorted to the bridal waiting room. Through the venetian blind, she spotted her mother at the door, anxiously waiting to welcome Himal's family with a prayer.

Anjani waited alone in the tiny white room. More hooters blared when Himal arrived. Her heart swelled, imagining him all dressed up and ready to marry her. She wondered if she could see him before he walked down the aisle. She flung the door open. She heard the singing and prayers begin. Himal must already be at the entrance. Aunty Dolly was waiting at the doorway of the little white room.

'No, Anjani, you can't see him now.' Aunty Dolly giggled and pushed Anjani back into the little room. 'You have to wait inside. It's not yet time for you to come out. I'll tell you when we're ready!' She closed the door on Anjani's laughing face.

Anjani stopped laughing and moved her hands away from her face. The mendhi on her palms formed intricate patterns in a deep, velvety red. The grandmothers of old were right. This love was profound. Today, fate had fulfilled Anjani's destiny.

A few minutes later they were both on stage with the priest reciting sacred mantras in Sanskrit.

'How could you keep it a secret from me that you went to visit my father?' Anjani whispered as they placed the special sandalwood mix into the havan.

'I didn't want you to get scared and change your mind about me.' Little did he know that all Anjani ever wanted was to be with him forever.

'You look handsome,' she said as another sandalwood mix left the palms of their hands and crackled in the fire.

'I had to make an effort for you!' said Himal.

They saw their internal laughter in each other's eyes. The bubble quickly burst when the priest glared at them and cleared his throat.

'Am I marrying myself? Pay attention to the mantras!' He clicked his tongue as they looked at him with doe eyes.

Anjani fought back fits of giggles through the rest of the ritual as her happiness radiated.

—

The fresh evening air cooled the bridal couple as they stood outside, ready for departure to the groom's home. Nirmala and Nanima were so pleased with their new son-in-law. Anjani wondered how she'd ever doubted their acceptance of him. But she'd had no part to play in convincing them. It was all male charm – her father's and Himal's.

For Nanima it seemed that Anjani and Surya had been little

girls just yesterday. She didn't want to let go of her granddaughter. She still wanted to wake her up in the mornings and answer her questions.

Nirmala was swollen with pride as she hugged Anjani. She had come to accept what happened to Surya, but she admired Anjani for her fierce tenacity and for never abandoning her family. Her daughters had grown up despite all her fears for them, and now Anjani was moving on to a new path in her life. Nirmala felt like the proudest mother on the planet.

In keeping with tradition, Surya gave Anjani a drink of water from a steel cup before allowing her sister to leave for her new home. She didn't want to cry. This was, after all, the happiest day for Anjani. Nevertheless, it felt like a partial closure of their relationship – their sisterhood.

Anjani knew what Surya was thinking and didn't want to let her go. 'I'll never be too far away or too busy for you, you know that?'

They stood there hugging each other. Mascara and kohl eyeliner streaked their faces. Surya couldn't find her voice but she released her hands from her sister and looked into her eyes. Their understanding didn't need words. Ashok walked up to them with Diya in his arms.

'Come here, my twinkle-toes,' said Anjani. 'Now you remember to bring your Mummy to visit often, OK?' Diya smiled at Anjani as she always did.

Anjani remembered the first moment she'd laid eyes on her niece. She still had a mystical golden glow. Surya reached out for her daughter, who burst into innocent tears. It seemed symbolic of the moment.

Ashok took Anjani's hand and placed it in Himal's.

'She is in your hands with our blessings. Look after her.' That was all he could say. It was time for his daughter to start a new phase of her life and she would always have his support and love.

Anjani's heart was ripped out of her chest. Himal held her hand all the way to their new home, but the tears continued. She was happy and smiled at him despite her tear-stained face. He understood.

'Now you look like one of those stars from Bollywood: tragic but beautiful. You are happy right?'

Anjani smiled back. 'I'm happy. Just sad. Oh, you know what I mean.'

EPILOGUE

Nanima felt differently these days, to say the least. Diya had wrapped her chubby fingers around her great-grandmother's heart and captivated her with her playful energy and pure spirit. Nanima could spend hours playing and entertaining her new love. Nothing put the child in a bad mood for too long. Her face glowed with carefree abandon and she had the ability to transfer her optimism to anybody who came into contact with her. That was what Nanima thought of this delightful little girl. It wasn't long before Diya spent some nights falling asleep next to her Par-Nani.

I'm in a mandir. It's so lovely and clean and bright. All the lights are on. The marble walls are shining.

'Arre Raam!' I bow down quickly.

I can't believe who I am bowing down in front of. Ganeshji. He's sitting there in front of me. Everything is shining. I can see his four arms. His elephant head with small eyes. What a blessing for me. Now even if I die tomorrow I can be in peace. Now that I saw Ganeshji. But who's that sitting on him?

They are so happy together. She is a little girl. What a pretty dress she's wearing. A pink and white one. She's also smiling and shining.

I'm so blessed to see this. She also puts her hand up, like all the God pictures in my mandir. She's blessing me. Wait, I think I know her.

It's Diya.

'Diya? Mera bacha, is it you?' She is shining so much now. I can't see Ganeshji any more and she is too bright also. So much light.

Nanima opened her eyes and let out a quick breath. Diya was sleeping soundly next to her. What a beautiful child she was. Ganeshji had come into Nanima's dreams. Not like those nightmares from last time. This time Ganeshji was happy and had given his blessing. And was that Diya? Nanima was sure of her dream. It was like a vision. Diya was a blessed child. Never mind how she had come into this world. There had to be something special about her. That's why she was such a good baby. She was God's child. Nirmala must take her to Guruji for blessing. They would all love her and protect her. Then one day, something big is going to happen with this child. This dream was proof.

Next to Nanima, tucked between layers of pillows and a fluffy pink and white blanket, Diya dreamed baby dreams and reconnected with her maker.

The End

GLOSSARY OF TERMS

aarti: Waving of lamps on a tray, performed at the end of every prayer session at a temple.

agarbathi: Incense used at prayer places and temples.

Arre Bhagwan/Arre Raam: Hindi expression of shock, taking the name of a Hindu deity, Lord Raam, or Bhagwan (which means 'God' in Hindi), for protection against the shock. Can loosely be compared to 'Oh God!' in English.

ayo: Tamil colloquial term of exclamation.

beti: Hindi word meaning daughter.

burfi: Traditional Indian sweetmeat made from milk powder, cream and almonds.

chatti: Traditional Hindu naming ceremony performed six days after a baby is born.

Devtas: Sanskrit term for Gods.

dhal: Lentil soup dish, which can be made from a variety of lentil types.

dharma: One's righteous duty in Hinduism.

dhoti: Piece of calico cloth traditionally worn draped around the legs by Indian men.

dolak: Traditional Indian drum.

Ganapatibapa/Ganeshji/Ganesha/ Avighna: Elephant-headed Hindu deity known as the remover of all obstacles.

Ganesh Chaturthi: Hindu festival celebrated annually to mark the birth of Lord Ganesha.

ghuusa: Hindi colloquial term for mischief.

Guj/Guji: Indian slang for Gujerati, a group of Hindus originating from Northern India, mostly from the state of Gujerat.

Guruji: Holy man or priest.

Havan: Sacred fire lit in a special four-sided, copper or brass pot used at most Hindu prayers performed with a priest.

hayibo: Zulu colloquial term of exclamation.

ja: Hindi word meaning 'go!'

jeera chilli papad: Disc-shaped snack made with flour and seasoned with red or green chillies and cumin seeds. Usually eaten as an accompaniment to Indian vegetarian food.

jhunda: Holy flags marking the external prayer place of a Hindu home.

kanna: South Indian term of endearment for a loved one.

karmasaathi: The Hindu belief in the journey of souls that reconnect as they take different lives. The souls that continually meet each other in different lives and bodies are known as karmasaathi.

khanya-dhan: Wedding-day ceremony where the parents of the bride officially give her hand in marriage to the groom and his family.

laddoo: Indian sweetmeat made from chickpea flour, icing sugar, ghee and food colouring.

Ma Parvati/Parvati Matha: Lord Ganesha's mother; wife and consort to Lord Shiva.

mandir: Hindi word meaning temple.

mantra: Sacred lines of Hindu prayer recited from holy scriptures.

matha: Hindi word meaning mother.

mendhi: Henna paste applied to the hands and feet of a Hindu bride before her wedding day.

mere bache/bacha: Hindi term meaning my children/child.

moongh dhal: Green lentil soup made from mung beans.

Mushaka: The demi-god mouse, also known as Kroncha that is the mount or vehicle of Lord Ganesha. It is said that the size of the mouse in comparison to the elephant symbolises the state that our egos should be in – i.e. very small – to overcome our earthly vices.

par-nani: Hindi term denoting maternal great-grandmother.

pooja: Prayer ceremony.

prasad: Blessed sweetmeats or fruits offered at prayers, in which devotees can partake after any pooja.

pundit: Priest

punjabi: Traditional three-piece Indian garment consisting of pants, top and scarf.

puri: Small round discs made of flour and ghee that are deep fried and served as an accompaniment to curries.

putr: Sanskrit term for son.

Raam: The seventh avatar (incarnate) of Lord Vishnu, who appeared on Earth to conquer evil in the form of the demon-king Ravana.

rakshasi: Hindi term for she-devil.

roti: Large, soft discs of flour and ghee, toasted on a griddle and served as an accompaniment to curries.

sharara/gharara: Traditional female Indian garment consisting of a long skirt, short or long blouse, and a long scarf that is draped around the body.

Shankara/Shiva/Shiv Bhagwan: One of the deities that make up the Hindu Trinity, known as the destroyer of evil or the 'Mahadeva' – God of all Gods.

therewa: A contraction of 'there you are', often used in Durban amongst the Indian population as colloquial English.

tulsi: Basil leaf, used in Hindu prayer ceremonies as a sacred offering.

vibuthi: Ashes that have been blessed by a traditional healer/holy person, used for protection and to ward off evil.

Varuna (Lord): Protector against evil dreams. The earliest reference to dreams in Hindu scriptures, found in the Rig Veda, state that prayer to Lord Varuna can protect a person against evil dreams, but also that Lord Varuna distributes good and bad dreams based on one's karma and the karma that one still has to experience in their current life.

ACKNOWLEDGEMENTS

I wish to offer my heartfelt gratitude to the following people, without whom this story would not have materialised. To Colleen Higgs at Modjaji Books: thank you for finding me, putting up with my endless questions and giving my story its voice. To my editors, Fiona Snyckers and Lauren Smith; special thanks for wrestling with my ideas to create order in my thoughts. To my amazing husband, Vimesh Madhoo; you've been my unwavering bedrock of support and motivation. You've helped me take the first steps in realising a dream for which I'm forever in your debt. Thank you for believing in me and loving me even when I spent hours fighting with fictional characters in my head.

And lastly, to all the readers of this book, I wish to share this message with you: whatever occurs in your life, both good and bad, all will come to pass. Feel your pain. Be one with it and then let it go to make room for the other side of the coin of life. Let the joy come in. Embrace it with all your being because we cannot appreciate joy without pain, love without anguish, and happiness without suffering. Embrace all that it means to be human while your emotions take you from season to season.

Printed in the United States
By Bookmasters